Declan The Kid Detective

KIDNAPPING OF THE DIAMOND EYES GINGERBREAD PENGUIN

Maggy Downey

Illustrator of book cover: Diane Kolar
Illustrations by Diane Kolar

Copyright © 2013 Maggy Downey

ISBN 10: 1490928243

ISBN 13: 9781490928241

Library of Congress Control Number: 2013912747
CreateSpace Independent Publishing Platform
North Charleston, South Carolina

*Thank you God for
Your amazing Grace.*

Chapters

✒ Prologue

Sitting in Samantha Tate's lush entertainment room, her best friends chatted non-stop about the movie they had just watched, *The Kid who Saved the World: Memoirs of Daniel Slater*, and about the secret Samantha had been so tight-lipped about for three months, if not longer.

"I already told you what I think. Samantha's one of the contestants in that kid's reality show, *Surviving in Alaska – If you Dare*," Christina said. "It's her favourite show."

"*Surviving in Alaska*?" Addison sounded doubtful as he sipped cream soda through a straw. "Chris, Sam can barely survive winters in Cherryfield, let alone Alaska."

"I think the two of you are way off." Javier placed the DVD jacket he'd been reading on the coffee table. "She's probably..."

"I'm baaack." Samantha appeared carrying a jumbo size fuchsia gift bag. She smiled at the group as she raised the bag, and then gently placed it on the floor, laying it against the wall.

"I'm so sorry I couldn't tell you about this sooner," she apologized to her curious guests. "Nana and I were asked not to mention this to anyone unless they were immediate family members and people we enlisted to help us with this project. As you already know, the Inspire Children to Read – Books Speak Volumes Gala is next month. We hope this event will raise a small fortune for the Cherryfield chapter. And one way we expect to do this is through our auction at the gala."

Blank faces stared back at her. "Ahh...Sam. What's in the bag?" Addison asked sarcastically.

Annoyed at his interruption and tone, she snapped, "Don't rush me! I'm getting to that." She paused for a few seconds to get her thoughts back together, and then turned her attention back to the group. "Anyway, as I was saying, the items donated will be auctioned off. All the money raised from the gala will go towards the Cherryfield chapter to help promote great books." She reached for the oversized bag and pulled something out. "Ta-daaa! This is my donation."

The silence was deafening. Seconds ticked by as three pair of eyes stared at the subject in question with their mouths in perfectly shaped Os. Samantha was the first to speak. "Well! What do you think?" She inched a few steps closer so they could get a better view.

With a sigh, Christina finally spoke, keeping her eyes fixed on the object. "It's simply breathtaking!"

And it was. At two feet tall, four pounds in weight and two inches thick, this was no ordinary gingerbread cookie. In fact, it was a gingerbread penguin. Its colouring from the neck down was in white confectionery frosting, the hands were licorice black with silver painted nails. The penguin's feet were adorned with golden brown shoes and fancy intertwined black and sliver laces, identical in colour to the three buttons sitting vertically on its white stomach. The face, like the shoes, was golden brown, but coated lightly with glittering gold sparkles. The mouth was a thin, slightly U-shaped layer of black frosting, and the nose was a transparent black upside-down protruding heart-shaped gummy the size of a small plum, with a rain of silver glitter locked in it. But it was the eyes, oh the eyes, they were the attention grabber. Outlined in glittering black crystals, the almond-shaped eyes held in their centres an octagonal, and very real, diamond. At the epicentre of these diamonds rested a black gem, otherwise known as a black onyx, the size of the tiniest bead on a friendship bracelet. Complementing the eyes were black crystal lashes and eyebrows. It was staggeringly beautiful, a creation of pure ingenuity.

"H...h...how did you and your nana find a cookie baking pan in the shape of a penguin, and in that *size*?" Addison stuttered, finally tearing his eyes away from the cookie and back to Samantha.

"Oh, Daddy's good friend, Stan, the owner of Stan's Jewellery, makes templates for the jewellery he designs. He said he would have no problem making the baking pan for us, we just had to provide him with the dimensions."

"It's amazing!" Javier inched closer to the edge of his seat to get a better view. "I've never seen anything like it."

"The crystals...the diamonds, they must cost a fortune," Christina added.

"They do," Samantha admitted. "They were donated by Starbright Crystals and Diamonds, the largest company of its kind in the world. We've been told this will increase the value of the cookie 100 times."

"Amazing! I don't know what 100 times means, but that must be a lot." Addison studied the cookie.

Knock, knock, knock. The door opened to reveal an older version of Samantha. "Hello! Hope you enjoyed the movie." Samantha's mother walked in. "I'm sure you'll enjoy these." She placed a tray with four glasses of milk and a plate full of cookies on the walnut-coloured coffee table. The cookies were identical to the giant one in Samantha hands, sans the diamonds, crystals and size. "Compliments of the chefs," Mrs. Tate beamed as she tucked stray fiery red locks from her ponytail behind her ear. "I would have brought more, but I don't want any of you getting sick. Your parents would kill me."

As she started to leave, there was another knock at the door. "Nicki," Mrs. Tate said jokingly as her friend's head popped in the room. "Hope you're not trying to get more cookies out of me."

"If only." Nicki Blake walked in carrying her daughter, Trisha. "Hey there!" she said to the group. "You're in for a treat with those, real yummy. Once you have one, you just can't stop, except for this one here, right, sweetheart?" She looked down at her eleven year old son Regan as she ruffled his dark blond hair.

"Yuck!" Regan scowled.

"I know," Mrs. Blake turned her attention to Mrs. Tate. "I just got a call from Carl. There's a car pile-up on the highway that doesn't look like it's going to clear up anytime soon. Since he can't move until it's gone, he won't be able to pick Lynette up from her tennis lesson. Sorry about this. We'll have to discuss the timetable for the Agricultural Exhibit another time."

"No worries. I'll email you the set-up of the exhibit, so that at least you'll have an idea of how it's going to look."

"Sounds good." Mrs. Blake started cradling her now restless and cranky baby. "Talk to you soon. Enjoy," she said to the children.

"Bye, Mrs. Blake," they said in unison.

"Bye, Sam." Regan waved at her. "See you Sunday."

"Sunday?" Samantha seemed puzzled. "What's going on Sunday?"

"You're coming over to my place to play the video game *Surviving in Alaska* with me, remember?"

Samantha had to think for a second. "Oh, that's right! I completely forgot about it. I'm sorry, Regan. I promised Christina I would go shopping with her and her mother on that day to help pick out a dress for her performance next month. Do you mind if we put it off until next week?" Samantha seemed genuinely upset about picking sides, but seeing the look on Regan's face made her feel even guiltier about her choice.

"No, I can't do that." She turned to Christina. "I made plans with Regan first. You're just going to have to go without me, sorry."

"Samantha, this is very important to me." Christina started to sulk. "I really need you there." She then turned to Regan. "Regan, please, please, please give Sam the okay to go shopping with me," she begged. "Please!"

"Okay, fine! But you both owe me," Regan agreed grudgingly.

"Thank you!" they both said in unison, and then smiled at each other.

"Sweetheart, we really have to get going." Mrs. Blake ushered her son out the door.

"Let me walk you to your car," Mrs. Tate offered.

When the door shut behind them, Addison couldn't contain his feelings about the cookie. "Wow! And wow! That's some cookie."

"Did you taste the ginger?" Christina examined the one in her hand. "I feel like there's a party going on in my mouth."

"It's unbelievable! My mouth feels like it's going to explode. My taste buds just can't get enough of this cookie," Javier said. "Sam, where did you..."

"Sammie honey...I think it's time you put that thing away," an older lady with strawberry blonde hair entered the room, "before it gets crumbled to death or even worse, Hope mauls it beyond recognition then decides to make a meal out of it."

"Ok, Nana. I'll be right back." Samantha snatched the bag and left.

"Do you think Sam will give us the recipe?" Christina wondered as she reached for her second cookie. "I would love to add this to my binder of ginger recipes and maybe make a variety of different shaped gingerbread cookies for the Eighth Annual Cherryfield Gingerbread

Festival. This recipe sure would outmatch any dessert Zoie makes." She bit into the cookie.

"I can't see why not," Javier answered. "My dad is searching for new recipes to sell at his café. I think he could use the ingredients from this recipe to make all kinds of desserts. He would make a fortune."

"Yeah, and my mom could use it in one of her cooking competitions. For sure she would win the grand prize for best baked goods." Addison placed his empty glass on a coaster.

"Well, I guess we'll soon find out." Christina looked at the opening door and then Samantha.

Samantha sat down on the love seat next to Javier and reached for the last gingerbread cookie and glass of milk. "I guess you guys like the cookies," she said, looking at the crumb filled plate.

"Sam, um…we were wondering, uh…we were wondering if you would give us the recipe." Addison rushed the last few words out.

Samantha began to tense up as she looked at the questioning faces. "You guys are my best friends in the whole world. But this recipe," she sighed, "is a family recipe that goes back 210 years. It's for family members only."

"But we're best friends! That's like family. Isn't that right, guys?" Javier asked his friends.

"Uh-huh! That's right!" Christina and Addison responded, nodding their heads.

"You know what I mean. Blood-related family. This recipe can only be shared with relatives. I wish I could, but my family won't allow it."

"I know what you mean." Christina looked at Addison and Javier. "It's like a family heirloom that's passed along from one generation to the next. It's just that yours happens to be a gingerbread recipe. You can't share a family heirloom with friends, no matter what it is. I understand, I really do," she said, as if trying to convince herself.

"Well, I don't! Ouch!" Addison yelled from Christina's elbow jabbing into his ribs. "I mean we do understand," he said, rubbing his side and giving Christina the evil eye.

"How do you get to have a recipe that's 210 years old?" Javier asked.

Samantha sighed. "It's a long story. I think we should go play Zooloretto."

"We want to know." Christina pleaded. "Please?"

Samantha sighed again. "Okay! But you better not fall asleep on me," she warned and began to tell the tale that had been told to her so many times before. "It was a gloomy period in Nuremberg, Germany, in 1801. The country still had not recovered from the thirty-year war that happened over 250 years ago. Disease and famine were widespread in the city, and most households had nothing. The few families that were just poor were considered blessed. My ancestral grandmother, G.G. Nana, came from such a family. Her and her husband Anton Hanns had two sons, Waldemar and Dietrich. To brighten the faces of her young children, she would experiment with baking different desserts. They loved them all, but there was one dessert they always wanted more than the rest, the ginger cookie. She always baked them in different shapes, until one day when uprooting ginger in her tiny backyard, she noticed a ginger root that was almost in the shape of a man. And it was at that moment she thought, 'Heureka! Like man this root came from dust, and like man this cookie will be made in his image. And she named it 'man of ginger cookie'."

Comfortable with storytelling, Samantha reclined on the loveseat and placed her forearm on the arm of the chair. "She then started making them for holidays and special family occasions. Soon after this, neighbours and friends learned of them and put in requests for dozens to be made. News of the cookie eventually spread throughout the city, and soon G.G. Nana couldn't keep up with the demand for them. So her husband managed the business side of things, and her two sisters, Angelika and Wilma, assisted her in baking and packaging the cookies. She then opened a bakery and named it Köstlich. In two years, G.G. Nana's name and the man of ginger were known throughout Germany, and in seven years throughout Europe."

"Yeah, right," Addison spat out. "You expect us to believe your ancestral grandmother was the founder of the gingerbread man? Come on, Sam, we weren't born yesterday."

Fury laced through her voice. "And why not?"

"Samantha, as you know, I'm something of an expert on the genealogy of gingerbread pastries." A sombre Christina crossed her legs. "The founder of the gingerbread man is Günther Gotthold Hanns, who happens to be a man."

"Ugh, gee!" Samantha rolled her eyes. "Christina, Günther Gotthold Hanns is G.G. Nana! My G.G. Nana! The initials G.G. stand for Günther Gotthold."

"Your nana was a man?"

Samantha slapped the palm of her hand to her forehead. "No Javier, she's a woman!"

"Then why does she have a man's name?"

"G.G. Nana's parents were told by a fortune teller that their next child would be a boy. Since they already had three girls, they were really excited about the birth of this child. G.G. Nana's parents decided on the first and second name for the baby months before she was born. When they learned the baby was a girl, they couldn't decide on any girl names and went with the names they had already chosen. From that day on, many people thought G.G. Nana was a boy."

"Wow! That's just crazy!" Javier took a sip of his milk. "Guess I won't be visiting a fortune teller anytime soon."

"I'm still confused." Addison frowned. "If what you're saying is true about your Nana discovering the gingerbread cookie and that awesome recipe, why isn't Köstlich a house-hold name like Chips Ahoy! or Nestle Toll House Cookies?"

"I can answer that," Christina cut in before Samantha had a chance to respond. "According to the book *The Ginger Man Empire: Triumph and Tragedy, Its Beginning, Its End*, he... I mean she," Christina corrected herself after receiving a scowl from Samantha, "made a for-tune from the recipe and lived a very privileged life with her family. It wasn't until many years after her death that Köstlich began to crumble. The book mentions her sons and how they sold the business to Dieter Christian Austerlitz, a wealthy businessman with a heart of stone, and how his mysterious death is believed to be con-nected to the cookie. It's an intriguing..."

"Chris, I have the book you're talking about." Samantha pulled it from the bookshelf. "I think they'll probably have a better understanding of what happened after reading the chapter 'The Fall of the Great Ginger Man Empire.' She flipped through the book. "Here we are!" she said and then read the tale.

When she finished, Javier reached for the book. "Amazing!" he said. "Especially when the stampede of fire in the shape of headless horses trampled D. C. Austerlitz to death. What a way to die." He shook his head.

Not fully convinced, Addison asked, "So if all the copies of G.G. Nana's recipe were destroyed and the ginger cookies from it were never made again, how did your family get it?"

"Her sons kept it! It was her legacy and an important part of their lives," Samantha said. "Just because they had no success running the family business, didn't mean they had no respect for what their mother built for them. According to the diary of Johanna Heidi Hanns Fleischer, the granddaughter of Dietrich Hanns, the brothers had come to an understanding that the recipe was only intended for G.G. Nana's success because her desire to bake the man of ginger cookie was for unselfish reasons, to bring joy and happiness to others. So it was agreed by the family that the recipe would only be used for family use and for charities. Since then, there have been no curses or mysterious deaths again."

"Sam, as creepy and spooky the story you just read to us is, I'm not a superstitious kid, so if that's what you're trying to protect us from, you don't need to worry," Addison assured her.

"Addison, I said no! No! No! No! Did you not hear anything I just said?"

"Enough!" Christina spoke up. "As much as I want this recipe, I believe Samantha when she says she can't share it with us." She paused for a second." We'll just have to respect her family wishes and let it go, Addison. Sam, that diary you mentioned of Johanna Heidi Hanns Fleischer, do you have it?"

"I do! I also have newspaper articles on G.G. Nana and D.C. Austerlitz when they were alive and shortly after their deaths. They're in the attic, and quite yellow because they're so old. Would you like to see them?"

"Great!" Javier closed the book at the chapter he was reading, 'Hands of a Master: How Günther Gotthold Hanns Made His Dough.'"

After they finished reading the newspaper clippings, Samantha went into her bedroom to get Zooloretto and then to the patio to play the game with her friends on an unusually warm autumn day.

Later that evening, hours after her friends had left, Samantha went upstairs to get ready for bed. Like any good shepherd watching over its sheep, she checked in on her edible penguin to make sure all was well, only to find it was gone.

Declan the Kid Detective

A slight wind from the north breezed through the backyard of 27 Newport Boulevard, causing a rainfall of loose autumn leaves to fall from trees onto the main house, its yard and the rooftop of a small oak shed nestled at the far end corner of the backyard. On the side of the shed, next to the door, was a cedar sign with the words "Declan McLeod Investigative Agency" carved in black. Just under that was his website address in smaller print. At the doorstep of the entrance lay a floor mat in the shape of a football on a greyish limestone walkway.

Inside the agency was, well, different. Like the outdoor floor mat, the indoor one was a football. Just next to the entrance was a blue and yellow safari coat hanger. The windows were decorated with animated colourful jungle animal curtains that had hung in Declan's bedroom for the first six years of his life. Against a wall sat a bookshelf with some books Declan had never read and many more he had read at least half a dozen times. Facing the bookshelf, on the other side of the agency, was a pastel blue chest drawer Declan's clothes used to live in. It was now used as a filing cabinet to store documents on his previous cases.

The centre of the floor had an area rug with a map of the world. Sitting on top of it was a football and soccer-themed bean bag chair that faced a medium-size brown oak desk and an oak wood chair behind it. On the wall just above that chair hung a painting of a man with short, wavy golden hair with traces of silver and amber eyes. The initials D.M.M were on the bottom corner. And beneath the painting sat an eleven-year-old boy with shaggy, curly, burned-gold blond hair, wide amber eyes and long golden lashes, a long face and a cleft in his chin.

Finishing up his latest case, Declan folded the invoice billed to Abdul Sarafpour into three columns, slipped it in an envelope, dipped a purple sponge into a water-filled McDonald's sauce cup, sealed it and then tossed it in a cardboard box marked "Outbox" to be delivered. He'd give it to Abdul at their next soccer practice.

He then reflected on the bizarre case. For two full weeks, Abdul had received large quantities of gerberas flowers every place he went. He found them in his school drawer, his locker in the boys change room, on his home doorstep and one time even under his bed sheets. What made this stalking case even worse was the fact that Abdul was allergic to gerberas. His swollen face had just now started to look normal again.

As it turned out, Katrina Petrov, a classmate of Abdul's, had a huge crush on him. She had left him her favourite flower as a way of expressing her feelings for him. Declan solved the case on a day he went to the post office with his mother. He saw Katrina there with a bunch of gerberas wrapped in newspaper around the stems. She was sending them by special delivery to 123 Court Avenue, Abdul's home address.

Declan glanced over at the stack of books sitting on the corner of his desk, sighed and then stared into space. He loved solving mysteries and unravelling things, whether it was a puzzle, mystery movies or his favourite television show, *Detective Cuomo*. He guessed that was probably one of the reasons he'd got into investigation.

Absently, he picked up the pile of books then placed them in front of him. With all his might, he focused his attention on the book in front of him and saw his next assignment stare right back at him. "I really don't want to do this," he sighed. He then forced himself to open that dreaded book he wished would just disappear, along with the all the expectations.

✌ Samantha's Dilemma

Deeply focused on his current assignment, Declan missed both the knock on his door and the opening of it. Startled as he looked up at the redheaded girl standing in his doorway, he almost missed her greeting. "Samantha?"

"Uh, your mom said I could come in. Umm... sorry, it looks like you're working on something really difficult. I could come back later if you like."

"Uh, that's okay. It's just French." He quickly shut the book. "I hate it, and I'm no good at it. My parents are thinking about getting me a tutor for it." He shook his head. "I don't know why we have to take this. It's not like I plan on moving to Québec or France. Come in. Sit down." He gestured to the bean bag chair. "So what's up?" he asked, seeing the worry on her face.

"I need your help in finding a missing gingerbread penguin cookie." She explained everything while Declan documented it all on his spring green-coloured laptop.

"So the last time you saw the penguin cookie was when you went in your bedroom to get the game Zooloretto?" he confirmed.

"That's right."

"And no one, except for Christina, Javier, Addison, your mother and grandmother, were in the house after that?"

He studied her sitting across from him. Her hair was wavy, just below her shoulders, her eyes green with a slight slant to them and right now a slight fear in them. He assumed the reason for that was because she knew what he was about to say. They'd known each other since grade one. He was also in her grade two and five classes, and they were both members of Inspire Children to Read. So he knew Christina, Javier and Addison were her best friends.

"Samantha, from everything you just told me, the thief is one of your friends."

"That's impossible! I don't believe it! I won't believe. They would never do anything like that to me. Never!" she said adamantly.

He knew that would be her response. "So are you saying you think your mother or grandmother took it?" He then raised a hand when she was about to speak. "I'm just trying to make a point. Your friends and family were the only ones at your place when the cookie disappeared. Both your mother and grandmother have the recipe and are also helping out with the fundraiser, so they would have no reason to take it. But from everything you just told me, your friends have motives," Declan continued as he reclined back in his chair. "And they had opportunity. Because, as you said, none of them were with you on the patio throughout the entire game of Zooloretto.

"Samantha, look," he sighed when he sensed her reluctance, "I can only base this case on what you give me. If there are other people you think might be suspects, and they were around your place at the time your cookie disappeared, please share. Otherwise, this case is built on three suspects, your best friends. If you don't want me to investigate them, then I can't take this case."

"Are you saying you will take this case?"

"No. What I'm saying is that I can't take this case if you don't allow me to handle it my way, and there are other things we have to agree on before I can commit."

"Like what?" She seemed puzzled.

"Like the service fee for my assistant and me. We don't investigate for free, and we need to pay for things like transportation and administrative services."

"Oh, yeah," she said, deflated. She looked down at her hands in her lap. "Well, I just spent my allowance. I have my savings for Christmas presents, but I really don't want to touch that." She paused. "Oh, I guess I have no choice but to... Wait! Wait a second. Didn't you say your parents are thinking about hiring a French tutor for you?"

He nodded.

"I could be your tutor for free. I get straight A's in French. In fact, it's one of my favourite subjects. I could tutor you in exchange for you taking on the case. As for transportation expenses, I think I can afford to take a few dollars away from my Christmas savings, how about that?"

"Sounds great, but what about Layla? She doesn't need a French tutor, or any tutor for that matter," Declan asked.

"Yeah that's right." Her voice went almost to a whisper as she knitted her eyebrows and tucked her hair behind her ear. "Layla needs to be paid as well. Let me think." There was silence in the little agency for seconds while Samantha concentrated. "Oh, I got it!" she cried out. "A digital music gift card! I got it for my birthday a few weeks ago. It's from Karl's Music. It's worth four downloads. How's that for payment."

Layla's a music lover, Declan thought. *There should be no problem there.* As for him, getting tutoring lessons from Samantha could work in his favour. With that extra money his parents would save in hiring one, maybe he could talk them into getting him a pair of Youth Predator PS TRX soccer shoes. He'd be the only kid on the field with them. He'd been dying to own a pair. "Sweet!"

"Great! So you'll take the case?"

"Ho...hol...hold on, Samantha. Not so fast," Declan cut in as he leaned closer to his desk. "The deal is not sealed yet."

"Huh?" She frowned. "Why not? You said you're fine with the fee."

"You'll hear no complaints from me, but you do need to understand that I'll only take this case if you allow me to handle it my way. Are you okay with that?"

"If I want my cookie back, I guess I have to be, so yes, I'm okay with that," she smiled.

"Okay, good." He smiled back. "Hey, wait a second," he said. "I still need to speak with Layla about this, but I can't see there being a problem."

"Oh, thank you so much, Declan." She started to get out of her seat, but stayed put when Declan motioned for her to stay.

"Before you leave, I have one more question. Did you bring any evidence with you?"

"Oh, yes, of course! I almost forgot." She reached for her knapsack and handed him a book and a picture of herself and her nana holding the jumbo gingerbread penguin with smiles as bright as the penguin's diamond eyes and two yellow Post-it notes.

"Wow!" Declan said in disbelief. "Look at the size of that cookie. It would take me at least a year to finish that off. That's some cookie." He placed the book and picture in front of him and read the notes.

'Won't hurt cookie, just want ingri-dients. I get back to you.'

Uh-huh, Declan thought as he looked at the pencil-written note. The sticky notes were small, yes, but there was no excuse for poor spelling and bad grammar. He then flipped to the second sheet.

'Don't tell grow-ups. Will crush it till crumbs like sand.'

Declan shook his head. As a member of the Inspire Children to Read, he took this theft personally.

"I found those in the bag the cookie was in," Samantha said. "That's the only evidence I have." She shrugged.

"Did you mention this to anyone else?"

She pondered that for a second. "Well, I did mention it to Regan. And I'm glad I did," she went on before he had a chance to scold her.

"It's because of him that I came to you. He said you found his golden retriever Moo Moo last year when she went missing. He said even the police couldn't find her."

That was true. He'd found Moo Moo curled up in the floor level cupboard of Lucky Ice & Cream Shop with ice cream all over her face, two days after he was asked to take the case. Apparently she had climbed onto the counter when no one was around and helped herself to the different tubes of ice cream. Her gluttonous behaviour caused her to vomit all over Declan's new running shoes when he bent down to pet her. He later learned that she loved ice cream, but Regan's parents said she was gaining too much weight and she'd been put on a diet. It wasn't one of his more memorable cases. "Okay then. Well, I can't get upset about that. But tell no one else. Got that?" he insisted.

"Can I at least tell my friends you plan to question them?"

"Giving them notice gives them time to prepare better lies. Samantha, you gave me your word, no tampering with this case."

"Yes, okay, I won't, promise!" She put a hand up to indicate just that. "Declan, I have less than a month before the gala, do you think you'll be able to find it by then?"

"I don't know," he said sincerely, knowing that wasn't the answer she wanted to hear.

"But what I can tell you is that out of all the cases I've worked on, there's not one I didn't solve."

"Well, I guess there's some relief in that." She gave him a weak smile.

Declan looked down on his desk at the book Samantha had given him, *The Ginger Man Empire: Triumph and Tragedy, Its Beginning, Its End.* "What's this for?"

"I thought this might help answer some questions you may have about the history of my family's gingerbread recipe. I'm not expecting you to read the entire book. I know how busy you are. But if you can, read chapter twenty-three, 'The Fall of the Great Ginger Man Empire.' That should answer some of your questions. "Oh, one more thing." She handed him four cellophane-wrapped gingerbread penguins. "These are for you and Layla."

"Oh." He smiled as he removed the cellophane from one of them. "Thanks!" And then he bit one of its legs off. "Mmm! Great cookie!" he said while still chewing on it. He then took a bite off the other leg before swallowing the first one. "I now understand why your cookie was stolen." He chewed a second longer to make sure most of the cookie was swallowed before speaking again. "This is one good cookie!"

An Afternoon at Latin Chisporroteo – Good Sweets & Eats

On the Cherryfield Zipp Transit bus, Declan and Layla Price sat at the very back reviewing the information and questions they had for their first suspect. Buses were the least productive place for them to get any work done, because Layla did not like them. In fact, she hated them. She complained about them every time they had to use one. If she didn't get a ride to where she was going, she would walk, if the travelling distance was within reason, before taking the bus.

Today, however, there were no complaints, thank goodness. It was probably because the person sitting next to her was a burly, tough-looking guy that smelled as if he had not had a bath in a week. Instead, her body was tilted towards his so that she rested on her hip, instead of her butt, while holding her notes.

At times it appeared as if she was going to pass out from holding her breath so long. He gave her little eye contact for fear of exploding into uncontrollable laughter. Instead he looked out the window at the vibrant fall colours on the trees and ground.

He then made the mistake of turning his head back to Layla, only to see her eyes trans-fixed by something. He followed her stare to a man in a brown leather coat and jean pants digging and digging in his nose. It was almost as if he was digging for something. And then, like that, he pulled it out. Declan could see the boogers, even from a distance. The man then rolled it between his thumb and finger, moulding it into a tiny ball, and flung it into the air. Like a shot he imagined only Kobe Bryant could make, it landed in the small opening of a cup of coffee another passenger was holding. Unaware of what had gone into her cup, the passenger took a few sips from it. It was surreal.

"I don't think I'll be able to eat for a week." Layla let her breath out for the first time since boarding the bus.

"Neither will I," muttered smelly guy next to her.

❧

As they got off the bus, Layla let her breath out for the second time since the ride. "There it is, Declan, Latín Chisporroteo – Good Sweets & Eats." She pointed to the café on the opposite side of the street, about half a block away. The slight breeze blew back her almost shoulder-length bushy, dark brown, tightly-curled little ringlets, leaving her chocolate-coloured skin exposed to the air. She wore a grey turtleneck and a grey pleated plaid skirt mixed with pink, white, black and pink tights and a pink and brown horizontal-striped rugby puffer vest. Declan's older sisters, Meghan and Kellie, called her a mini fashionista.

Latín Chisporroteo – Good Sweets & Eats Café was in a little box-shaped brick house. The patio had tables, chairs and presently no guests. Around it were black iron bars with a gate that reached just above Declan's waist.

Inside, the first thing he noticed, or heard, was the pulsating music of Anthony Vega, the number one international salsa singer in the world, on the stereo speakers. He looked around and could see Halloween decorations. At the back of the café was a teenager sitting in a comfy chocolate-brown living room chair with his laptop on his lap, a stack of books on a table, his knapsack and computer case sitting in an identical chair next to him and a iPhone to his ear. It was Brett, the lifeguard from the Cherryfield Community Centre. He was the only guest in the café. *Does he ever stop talking on that iPhone?* Declan wondered.

Layla, an expert on dining out, said anytime between 2:00 and 4:00 p.m. would be a perfect time to visit Javier Gómez at the café, because business was usually slow around this time.

The door leading to the kitchen swung open and a man appeared. He was tall and slender and had short, straight jet-black hair and a goatee. He had an apron wrapped around his waist with three pockets; one had a small black leather case in it. "*Buenas tardes mis niños,*" Luis greeted them in Spanish. "What brings the two of you to this end of the city?" He put the tray of clean dishes on the counter.

"Ummm...we...um want to interview Javier for an assignment we're working on about kids at work," Declan lied. "Yeah, is he here?"

Luis eyebrow shot up as if sceptical about the reason. "Is that so?"

"Yep, that would be true," Layla put in, coming to Declan's defence. "We know a few kids that...ah...help out at their parents' businesses.

And...ah we want to know what that's like...to work...as a kid," she added.

"Okay, if that's the case, Javier is the perfect person to speak with. He's a tremendous help and a hard worker, but he only works a few hours on the weekends. I hope that's enough." When the children nodded, he called out, "Javier, *viene aquí. Allí un par de sus compañeros de clase aquí a hasta la vista.*"

Javier appeared a few seconds later wearing attire almost identical to his father's. Like his father, he had short, straight black hair and a slender build. He was tall for his age, although not quite as tall as Declan, and had hazel eyes. From what Layla had uncovered about him, Javier and Samantha had been friends since they were in daycare.

His mother had left his dad, himself and his younger sister Galena three years ago and had never been in touch with them since. He was not involved in many after school activities, except for karate classes on Tuesdays and Spanish lessons every Thursday. "Hi! What's going on?" He gave Declan a suspicious look and completely ignored Layla.

"Hi! Javier...umm..." Not quite knowing what to say while Luis was standing there, Declan stuttered on. "Can...could we...ah...talk to you about a school assignment?"

"Uh, sure." Javier looked confused. "Dad, is it okay that we sit on the patio?"

"*Fino!*" His dad looked back and forth between Javier and Declan. "Just don't forget you have to get back to work by three o'clock. We have to finish putting up the rest of the Halloween decorations and set the dessert samples out for our guests." He turned his attention to Declan and Layla. "Tell you what, *mis niños*, you will be my first testers for today. I'm going to bring the two of you a tray of desserts to sample."

❧

"How many hours of work do you put in a week?" Layla asked Javier as they sat on the patio.

He paused for a moment, looking uneasy. "Three hours on Saturdays and Sundays. But I'll be working longer today because I want to help with the decorations." He then turned his attention to Declan. "So what's your real reason for coming? You've never needed my help with assignments."

"Your best friend Samantha hired us to find her missing gingerbread penguin she planned to donate to Inspire Children to Read." Declan paused for a second to gauge Javier's reaction. He got none. "It was stolen."

"Oh, I didn't know that. I can't believe she kept that from me for a full week." He seemed surprised.

"How do you know it was stolen a week ago?" Declan studied him.

"Ah, didn't you just say it was stolen a week ago?"

"No, he didn't," Layla answered. "So how did you know?"

"Umm..." Javier gave a weak, embarrassed laugh, "it was just a guess."

"It was stolen one week from yesterday. That's some guess," Declan said dryly, looking him dead straight in the eyes. He then went into his knapsack, pulled out an envelope and handed it to Javier. "Have you seen this before?"

"No!" Javier said quickly then handed the yellow Post-it notes back to Declan.

"Do you think this is something one of your friends might have done?" Declan asked.

"Of course not," Javier answered in annoyance.

"Look what we have here!" Taken by surprise, the children's heads whipped in the direction of the voice and noticed Luis carrying a tray above his shoulder with one hand. "A reward for you hard working kids." He opened the tray stand and placed the tray on it.

It was a kid's lottery win in a bakery shop. The platter Luis placed on the centre of the table had too many choices. Declan decided he must have one of everything. Hadn't Luis said he wanted them to be his first testers? It would be an insult if they did anything else.

After Declan piled his plate with edible spooky sweets, he took a sip from a tall, slim glass with green, slimy fruit punch on the inside, whitish green froth foaming at the rim and cherry syrup drizzled on the side.

"Wow! Would you look at this?" Layla held up a tarantula cookie covered in chocolate, the earlier incident on the bus temporarily forgotten. "Javier, you are sooooo lucky to have a dad who can bake desserts like this. The only dessert my mother can make is a smoothie." She bit into one of the tarantula's legs. "Do you get to eat like this all the time?

"Well, no." Javier blushed as he looked into his lime punch. "My dad is very strict about what Galena and I eat. We only eat this stuff a few times a week," he said, giving his full attention once again to Declan.

Irritation flickered over Layla's face at this last snub, Declan noticed. She then took an angry bite into the tarantula, chewing its head into bits, then turned away from the conversation and looked into space.

Guess I'll be the only one interrogating Javier, Declan thought. "Great gingerbread cookie." He held up the cookie with its decapitated head. "Not nearly as good as Sam's, but good enough to eat, which reminds me of why we're here. Do you think the recipe for Samantha's gingerbread cookie would help bring back some of those guests your father lost?"

Insulted, Javier shot back. "My father is a baker. He doesn't need anyone's recipe to attract guests to his café."

"Oh, I won't argue with you there, but with a recipe like Sam's, he could have people from all over the country ordering them. He would be rich. Just like Mrs. Fields."

"Business may be a little slow right now, but it will pick up again. It always does."

"It must be tough for your father being a single parent of two. I'm sure you would do anything you could to help make things easier for him," Declan said with a trace of sympathy, leaning forward.

"I wouldn't steal, if that's what you're saying. I especially wouldn't steal from my best friend." Javier raised his voice.

"Hmm…" Declan paused for a second to give that some thought. He looked over at Layla and saw she was taking notes, as she usually did when they questioned suspects. "So the evening the cookie went missing, the same evening you were at Samantha's place and begged for the recipe, you didn't steal it?"

"No, I didn't."

"You weren't tempted to steal it after Samantha refused to give it to you?"

"Not in the least." Javier plopped a marshmallow ghost into his mouth.

Liar, Declan thought. "You don't expect us to believe that, do you?"

"I don't care what you believe. I didn't do it! Plus I was with Samantha the entire time, so how could I have taken it?"

"Oh, I'm glad you brought that up, because that's not what Samantha told me." *Liar again,* Declan thought, reaching for a spider web butter tart. "In case you forgot, there was that one time in the backyard when you were playing Zooloretto, and you said you had to go to the washroom. You mentioned something about your aching tummy and that your friends shouldn't worry if you take a little longer getting back. Do you remember now?"

Averting his eyes from Declan, Javier grabbed an eyeball cupcake and began peeling off the wrapper. "Oh yeah, I remember now. I needed sometime alone for the pain to go. It must have been from the gingerbread cookie. I had a bad reaction to it. I...umm went into the medicine cabinet, took a child's Tylenol and then got some water from the sink with my hands to rinse it down. And, uh...then I sat on the toilet seat until I felt better."

"So you only went back with your friends after your stomach felt better?" Declan glanced at Layla. She took a brief break to take a bite of a black cat s'mores cookie.

"You see something wrong with that?"

"Well, I do have a problem with the pain you said had come and gone so quickly. Usually when I take a pill to relieve pain in my stomach, it takes at least a half an hour to go away, not a few minutes." Declan took another sip of his drink. "By the way, how long were you in the washroom?"

"How would I know? It's not like there's a clock in there or something."

"Javier, I'm curious," Layla said, finally breaking her silence, "after your pain had gone so quickly, weren't you an eenie, weenie, beenie bit tempted to have one last peek at that amazing cookie, a cookie that was made with the ingredients from the founder of the gingerbread cookie?

"I didn't go into Sam's bedroom!"

"I didn't say you did." Layla's cat-shaped eyes widen in surprise at Javier's response.

"Ohh." He paused, almost as if trying to think of what next to say. Declan then noticed his puzzlement slowly turning to frustration. "Look, I can't help you!" He turned on Declan. "I've got to help my father now. You've taken up enough of my time already."

"But it's not three o'clock yet." Layla looked down at her watch.

"Don't bother me about this anymore," Javier said, ignoring her comment.

At that moment, the café door swung open. "Yeah, we met them back stage after the concert. Like, that was completely real! I was like, hey... this is what a rock concert should be, gimmie more!" Brett let out a low laugh while walking to his little worn-out two-door teal car. The kids watched him as he tucked his iPhone in his pocket and then drove off.

Declan stared at the car until it was no longer in sight. He then turned back to Javier. "Thanks for your time, and thank your dad for the treats." He flashed an ever-so-pleasant smile as he stood up. "Oh, and about keeping in touch with you, if we find any evidence that leads us to you, we'll be back. Happy decorating," he added when he noticed Javier was set to argue, and then walked off.

"Arghhhh! Did you see that, Declan? How he ignored me! Did you see it?" Layla ranted.

Playing it cool, Declan asked, "Did you say anything to him in the past to make him upset with you?"

"Of course not." Layla frowned. "I barely know him. He probably has a problem with me questioning him because I'm a girl. Gee," she shook her head, "all the strides women's lib has made for girls and there are still some boys who don't see us as equals. Well, if he stole that gingerbread penguin, I'll show him just how equal we are."

"But if he thought like that, Christina and Samantha wouldn't be his best friends," Declan pointed out as they walked to the bus stop.

"Well, if he stole the cookie, he's not really their best friend," she shot back.

Declan opened his mouth to make a response but realized he didn't have one. He shook his head and lightly waved a hand in the air.

"Sometimes at school, I catch him staring at me and then when I stare back, he turns away and pretends everything is normal. Now do you see what I mean?"

"*Now* I do." And he did.

✐ Addison Got Game

Sitting in the stands at the Cherryfield Public School gymnasium, Declan watched his school basketball team practice for its first game of the season. He didn't particularly care for the sport. It was too boring for his taste, and points seemed too easy to get without much effort. Soccer and American football were his games.

"Awwwsome!" Pradeep bellowed. "I just love this game. Don't you wish you could shoot hoops like that?" he asked Declan.

"If only." Declan looked to the court with a pained expression. How much more of this game and Pradeep's constant play-by-play commentary could he take, he wondered. And where was Layla? What was taking her so long? She knew how much he hated this game — how could she leave him sitting here alone like this when he needed her most? It was times like these that he wished he had a iPhone, but his parents said it was out of the question because he was too young.

"Oh, Declan, there you are," Layla panted as she made her way through the aisle. "I'm so sorry I'm late. I completely lost track of time while I was instant messaging my cousin Terri. She said her and her family are having so much fun in Venice, Italy. She can't get over the fact that people only travel by water. She said they even have taxi boats that take you to wherever you want to go. Isn't that cool?"

"Anything's cooler than this."

"Yeah, I guess so. Hey listen," she lowered her voice for Declan's ears only, "could we find somewhere a little more private to talk about our next suspect before we meet with him?"

"Yes! Yes!" Pradeep shouted as he got to his feet to cheer. "Addison's the best! Isn't Addison the best? Man, he shoots hoops like chickens hatch eggs."

With gaping mouths, Declan and Layla could only stare at Pradeep. "Good idea," Declan responded.

❧

A few feet from the stands, Declan and Layla sat on the gymnasium floor as they mapped out their now nearly two-week-old case and their investigation of Addison Dalton. Like his friends, Addison was in grade six. He was a B student and captain of the Cherryfield Cheetahs basketball team, a title he'd received just this season based on his electrifying performance on the court last year. Entertaining to watch, he'd scored the most points last season and almost single-handedly won the team its first championship ever. However, the most interesting piece of information Layla uncovered from her research on Addison was that his mother competed in several different cooking contest each year, and that her next one, in January, was a dessert contest.

"Why does she compete in so many of them?" Declan asked as he skimmed through the sheets of data.

"I guess so she can win prizes and get on television cooking shows like *Dragon's Kitchen.*" Layla shrugged. "Could you imagine what it's like to be on that show? Pasty the head chef throwing your meal at the wall because you didn't put enough salt in it or yelling at you in front of everyone and calling you an idiot because the colour of your soup is orange instead of green. I've even seen a few of them cry and say they were never coming back because they were treated so mean."

"Great practice, guys!" Mr. Latimer, coach of the Cheetahs basketball team, walked across the court to congratulate his players. "Keep that up and we'll be looking at trophy number two real soon." A roar of cheers and applause erupted, followed by the basketball home team chant:

"Cherryfield Cheetahs, rock, rock, rock!
Duck and bend to avoid the block!
Shoot that ball then make 'em stop!
Cherryfield Cheetahs!!!"

The spectators continued this litany as Mr. Latimer pleaded with the fans to hush. When they did, he continued his speech. "This is the best basketball team Cherryfield elementary school has ever had! And you," he stretched his arm out to the audience, "are the best fans ever. We're going to win this season's championship for you!" The noise that had died down grew even louder than before. "Let the games begin!"

About thirty minutes later, Declan and Layla greeted Addison as he walked out of the boys change room. "Hey Addison," Declan called out, "great game!"

"Oh, hi Declan, Layla," Addison responded while adjusting his knapsack on his back. "Thanks. We really want to win two championships in a row. That would be a first in any sport for Cherryfield, and it would make Mr. Latimer so proud."

"Addison, we need to speak with you for a few minutes, do you have time?"

"What's up?" He combed his straight chestnut brown hair away from his face with his fingers.

"It's about Samantha's gingerbread penguin," Layla said. "It was stolen."

"What? It was stolen? How did that happen?" Addison's blue eyes widened.

"That's what we would like to know." Layla took on a more serious tone.

"Really." Addison took on the same tone. "So let me guess, the next question you're going to ask me is did I steal it, right?"

"Well, did you?" she asked.

"If I say no, will you leave me alone and go home?"

"Addison, we've been hired to find the cookie. Samantha says you are her best friend. If you didn't steal the cookie, what are you afraid of?" Layla demanded.

Addison wiped the beads of sweat off his forehead and paused for a few seconds. It was almost as if he was searching for the right words to say. "Nothing, and no, I didn't steal the cookie."

"Okay, fine. Thanks! Well then, I guess we'll be seeing you," Declan concluded with a smile.

"Is that it?" Addison seemed puzzled that he was being let off so easily.

"Um-hmm," Declan nodded. "You said you didn't take it, so what more is there to ask?"

"Uh, well nothing, nothing," Addison said awkwardly. He then made way to leave. "Bye."

"Oh, Addison, aren't you the least bit curious about when the cookie went missing, or do you already know that?" Declan shouted to him.

Addison stopped in his tracks then slowly turned around. "What's that supposed to mean?"

"Well, in case you don't know," Declan continued as if Addison had said nothing, "it was stolen on the day Samantha showed you the cookie. Remember now?"

Addison went silent.

"I thought since you and Samantha are best friends — you would want to know when it was stolen. She is your best friend, right?"

"How could I walk out the door without someone seeing me carrying that enormous cookie? Anyway, I couldn't have taken it. I was with Sam, Chris and Javier the entire time. Sam's mother even walked me to the door when I left."

"Now that's not true and we both know it," Layla corrected him. "You left your friends to go to the washroom. And as for that enormous cookie, there are so many ways you could've got it out of the house without anyone spotting you that I can't even count them."

"Okay, so I went to the washroom, big deal! Does that mean I stole the cookie?" he asked, completely unperturbed.

"I'm told your mother has a baking competition coming up a few months from now," Declan said. "Is it true that the grand prize is not only money, and a lot of it from what I was told, but a one-year contract with Pleasure Treats to manufacture and distribute the winner's dessert?"

"Wow! You really do your research." Addison seemed genuinely impressed.

"Thank Layla for that one." Declan smiled at her then turned his attention back to Addison. "The ingredients to that cookie would win your mother the grand prize. I know it and so do you. I know Sam's your friend, but I'm sure you would like to see your mother's own line of cookies on the grocery shelves. Gee, I know I would." Declan pressed on. "Addison, you have a strong motive, you have opportunity. It doesn't look good for you. Just confess!"

Addison closed his eyes and remained silent for a few seconds before he answered. "I confess! I wasn't completely truthful about going to the washroom."

Declan and Layla's eyes almost popped to the ground over the admission. Declan had never solved a case by simply asking the suspect to confess. He usually had to have the evidence to support his suspicions before the individual would admit to the crime. This was very new to him.

"Uh...well then...ah...Addison, we know this must be hard for you, but you'll feel better about it. Confessions are good for the soul. Well, that's what my dad always says," Declan said.

"I went to the washroom as I said I did, but while I was there, I just couldn't get that cookie off my mind," Addison reflected. "The taste of it was like a gingerbread cookie, but different and so much better than I've ever tasted before. It made me think about my mother's baking competition and what having the recipe would do for her. It was so good, so perfect. I could still taste it when I washed my hands. I almost knocked the insulin pen cartridge on the sink counter into the toilet when I reached for a towel to dry my hands, from daydreaming about it.

"After I left the washroom, I decided to go to Sam's room just to get another look at it. When I walked in, there it was, lying on her bed inside that huge bag. I sat on the bed next to it and pulled it out. It was then that the thought about stealing the cookie and using it as ransom to get the recipe." His face went slightly red over the admission as he averted his eyes.

Stealing was stealing, and Declan had no sympathy for those who did it, but a part of him admired and respected Addison for his in-your-face honesty. Here was one of the top athletes, if not *the* top athlete, of Cherryfield Elementary School, liked by everyone, on the verge of ruining his reputation by admitting to doing something terribly wrong to his best friend. It took a lot of courage to confess something like this. Especially when so little pressure had been used to get it.

This was the easiest case he'd ever worked on. In fact, it was so easy that he was almost disappointed he didn't have the challenge of solving the case by gathering clues and piecing them together, like he did for most of his cases.

"But I couldn't do it," Addison said, turning his eyes back to Layla and Declan. "I just couldn't do it! Sam's one of my closest friends, and stealing that gingerbread cookie would ruin our friendship. Plus it's just..."

"Wait a minute," Declan interrupted. "Did you just say you didn't take the cookie?"

"Yeah."

"But you just admitted to wanting to take the cookie to use as ransom for the recipe." Declan couldn't believe what he was hearing. "How could you admit to something like that and then say you didn't do it?"

"Easy. I didn't do it!" Addison's ever–so-cool exterior was crumbling into frustration. "Declan, just because I thought about stealing the cookie doesn't mean I stole it. Look, I'm not proud of myself about this, but I didn't steal the cookie."

"So you expect us to believe you were so tempted to steal the cookie that you went into

Samantha's room planning to do just that, but then your conscience got the better of you, so you decided against it? Addison, you're asking a lot from us," Declan smirked.

"I'm asking nothing from either of you. I didn't steal the cookie. Whether you believe me or not, I don't care."

Declan shimmied his knapsack off and pulled out a zip lock bag with two yellow Post-it-notes. He handed it to Addison.

"You think I wrote this?" Addison asked after reading it. He appeared to be shocked at its contents.

"Well, Addison, isn't it a little odd that what you just told us about using the cookie as ransom to get the recipe is exactly what these notes state," Layla demanded. "I mean what are the chances of that?"

"I didn't do this!" Addison re-read the notes. "Why would I confess the way I just did if I...if I did this?"

"I don't know. Maybe to throw us off track so that we would think you didn't do it for the reasons you just mentioned. Hey, Addison," Layla added when he started to laugh, "you have to admit, what are the chances that what you just told us matches with what's written on these?" She gestured to the yellow notes.

"I've had enough of this." Addison handed the notes back to Declan. "I have to go. My dad's probably wondering what happened to me. Thanks for completely wasting my time."

"Our pleasure." Declan placed them back in the zip lock bag. "And thank you for your time. We learned a lot about you. I just hope for your sake you didn't take the cookie. We'll be in touch."

"Please don't." Addison walked off.

Layla waited until he was out of sight. "Do you believe him?" she asked as she put her steno notepad into the side compartment of her knapsack.

"I don't know. Both Addison and Javier have very good motives and very weak reasons for why they didn't do it." Declan zipped up his navy blue goose down jacket as they walked to the foyer. "But I do have to wonder why Addison would admit to something like this if he did it. Why would he risk implicating himself?"

"For the same reason I just mentioned, to throw us off balance and convince us to think exactly the way you are, that he couldn't have done it because he's been so open and honest with us about wanting to. Declan, his mother has entered a contest where she is this close," she put her thumb and finger together leaving a little space between them, "to having her winning dessert sold in grocery stores across the country. Don't you think he would want that for his mother? He knows what that would do for her. And she probably wouldn't have to enter any more of those contests."

He knew what Layla said made sense, but he still had a problem with Addison's admission. If he'd done it, why come out and tell them he almost had? Why not try to cover up what he did? It wasn't like Layla and he would have been able to detect his thoughts. He needed time to think this one through. "I'm going to need to speak with Christina to get a better picture of exactly what happened." He looked out the foyer window. "This is one meeting I'm not looking forward to."

"I hear you. Do you want to bet Christina is going to say she didn't do it?"

"My allowance isn't large enough to bet against the obvious. Oh, there's my mom. Let's go!"

The Ginger Man Empire: Triumph and Tragedy, Its Beginning, Its End

Declan, Layla and Nigel had just wrapped up their time together at the Cherryfield Public Library working on their science project about hot air balloons. It was fascinating how they functioned. Moving it up and down basically required an increase in heat from its burner and a decrease for it to fall. To move it from place to place, you simply moved up and down, depending on the wind and what direction you wanted to take it in, and then rode with the wind. In 1999 a world record was set for the first around-the-world flight. It took 19 days, 21 hours and 55 minutes for two pilots to travel from the Swiss Alps in Switzerland to the North of Africa.

Declan sat in the library, minus his friends, so that he could steal some alone time to read the book Samantha had left with him, *The Ginger Man Empire: Triumph and Tragedy, Its Beginning, Its End.* He flipped it open to the chapter he'd inserted a bookmark in, "The Fall of the Great Ginger Man Empire." This was the chapter Samantha had asked him to read, if he could read no other. And he couldn't. He was simply too busy with soccer and swimming practices and the Inspire Children to Read book club. Oh, and how could he forget, his school-work, which he noticed he was getting more of since being in grade six. He couldn't wait until he didn't have to go to school anymore. It seemed like it was taking forever for that to happen. Oh well, what little time he had now was being spent on this case, and right now this chapter. He started to read:

The Fall of the Great Ginger Man Empire

(By Hanna Heintz – 1851, excerpt
translated in English)

Young and old mourned the death of Günther
Gotthold Hanns. The date of funeral was June 6,
1832. As a show of respect to this truly gifted
and generous human being, who not only contributed to the wealth and fame of Germany,
but helped it regain a sense of pride as a nation,
he was given a state funeral. Attendees included
citizens of Nuremberg, government officials of
Germany and Europe, British royalty and even
the Pope of Rome. During his eulogy, friends
and family spoke highly of him and his accom-
plishments. The only odd thing about these

speeches was that they kept referring to him as her. It made no sense.

For a brief period after his death, business at Köstlich remained as usual thanks to Günther's sons Waldemar and Dietrich, who inherited both their father's business and fortune. But they became restless, grouchy and bad-tempered with their customers and each other. Their change in temperament had very little to do with the death of their father, who they were saddened to lose, and more to do with the fact that they did not care to run the family business but felt an obligation to their deceased father to do so. Slowly, the production of the cookies declined. Like the decrease in cookies, the taste and quality were not to be desired. Depending on the day of the week, they would taste like anything from a bowl of sugar to a piece of cardboard.

Waldemar, the rebel of the two brothers, was seen regularly at the local tavern drowning his misery and hate for baking in whisky. Coming in to work one day from his binge with only two hours of sleep, Waldemar placed two full trays of cookie dough into the kiln for baking. Because he had little sleep and was not completely sober from the previous night, he accidentally used the oven door as a resting place for his head and arm and fell asleep while standing. Shortly afterwards, he woke up to a searing pain from the fire that had started on his shirt sleeve and had gone to his entire right arm and some of his hair. The burns, which were severe, would have been worse had Dietrich not come into the bakery when he did and extinguished the fire. From that moment on, Waldemar never ate or baked ginger cookies ever again.

Dietrich, Günther's youngest son, spent his childhood eating the ginger cookie as often as he could. He would scrape the meagre dough left in the bowl his father used to mix the batter to eat. He would even sneak cookies from the cookie jar whenever he got an opportunity, which was often. His obsession with the ginger cookie grew so great that he eventually ate them on a daily basis. It was because of this daily habit that Dietrich eventually grew to hate the taste of the ginger cookie. Even the smell of it would make him want to throw-up. It was for this reason as an adult he rarely worked at the bakery. Nevertheless, on one of those rare occasion, Dietrich removed a tray of cookies from the oven to place them on a rack to cool off, but distracted by the unusually strong aroma of the freshly baked ginger cookies, he didn't notice the splat of egg white on the floor and flipped onto the ground face first, onto the piping hot cookies. He suffered a broken nose that left a permanent bump the size of a cherry, and a dislocated baby toe.

With this streak of bad luck from running their father's business, Waldemar and Dietrich decided to sell the bakery to a local business tycoon, Dieter Christian Austerlitz, or as he was known to the community, D.C. Austerlitz.

D.C. Austerlitz was a clever and ambitious man who had a heart of stone. He knew how to build a business and recognized a good one when he saw it. For this reason, he wanted Köstlich. He knew he could build on its success to make it an empire of bakeries that would last forever. He had pressed the Hanns brothers to sell it to him shortly after their father's death, knowing they would turn down the offer, as they did. According to his only friend, Joselm Niemann, "Dieter was a man who got whatever he wanted, and he wanted Köstlich. He didn't believe the boys had the capability to run a business and said they would drive it into financial ruin. So he decided to wait it out. And to his relief it wasn't long. Early in 1834, Köstlich was on the brink of going out of business. Customers of the bakery were dissatisfied with the service and the taste of the man of ginger cookie, and no longer bought them. It was then that Dieter approached the brothers for a second time with the exact same offer, and this time they agreed, giving him the secret recipe of the man of ginger cookie, the bakery and a legacy."

Building on the success of the man of ginger cookie, Dieter decided the cookie needed a family and a home, and made ginger women and houses. This ignited a revival in the ginger cookie the country never expected to experience again. Customers were enjoying the cookies like never before. The ginger house, decorated effervescently with candies and chocolates, became a tradition on special occasions and holidays.

June 12, 1836, was declared the first national holiday for the man of ginger cookie, and a parade was held in celebration of this great day. The anthem, "My Long Lost Gingy has Come Back to Me," was a love song dedicated to the return of the man of ginger cookie and was sung annually on this day. (For lyrics to this song and others, refer to Chapter 26, page 439: Songs and Praises – Musical Tales of the Ginger Cookie.)

Imitators of the ginger cookie were forced out of business due to poor sales, giving D.C. Austerlitz a complete monopoly over the ginger cookie business and leaving him on the brink of building a baking dynasty. He could taste the success and the power, and he wanted it. With it he would be unstoppable and able to pay back those who had made fun of him as a child when he walked with a limp due to one leg being shorter than the other. They had played practical jokes on him as a teenager and refused to be his friend. The pain never left him nor had the names of the people who ridiculed him. This made him bitter and mean-spirited. Children were not allowed in his bakery because of the memories they brought up of his own childhood. And with all his wealth he never gave one penny back to help the poor and underprivileged. His only thoughts were of himself and his vengeance towards those who hurt his feelings. Joselm Niemann recalls what D.C. Austerlitz's said about his planned revenge. "We were fishing one afternoon, and out of nowhere Dieter mentioned the insults he had received as a child from other children and how they made him feel worthless and weird because of his limp leg. 'It was unfair,' he said. 'What did I do to them to make them hate me so much? Why wouldn't they be my friend; why wouldn't they stop picking on me?' he demanded almost hysterically. 'Well I'll fix them. I'll fix them all,' he went on as if it had just happened. 'They don't know this, but I'm within reach of releasing my wrath on all of them. And when that time comes, they will wish they never knew my name!' The tone in his voice sent chills up my spine. It was frightening! I knew to some degree he was a disturbed man, but I never knew how much until that moment."

❧

On October 13, 1840, D.C. Austerlitz was in his field on hands and knees worshipping his crops of ginger roots when he heard a faint sound like a trumpet. Ignoring this, he went back to praising his harvest. Minutes later, a thunderous trampling began to shake the ground. Austerlitz turned to the direction of the sound as he clutched a ginger root. He was paralyzed by what he saw. A blaze of lightning flashed across the horizon where the roaring came from. Following it was what appeared to be fire in the shape of a herd of winged head-less horses descending from the sky. They each had a pair of crystal white eyes and eyelashes on each wing and a wheel saw on the tip of their tails that spewed out a trail of blazing fire.

There was a cry from afar, pleading with D.C. Austerlitz to run, but he just stood there as if he was rooted to the earth. As the herd approached him, an apparition of a man's face appeared in the dark sky and then vanished. The headless horses then ascended into the sky and disappeared, as told by Wolf V. Haassenkamp, a witness to the entire incident a short distance away on his home porch. "I could see the headless horses charging towards him at full speed. I shouted out to him to 'run, Dieter, run,' but he just stood there. Seconds later, the field was quiet again and the stars were bright in the sky as if nothing happened only seconds ago. I hurried to D.C. Austerlitz's field and found his body trampled to death and burnt to a crisp along with his crop of ginger roots and his home. It was a sight that I have never gotten over to this day, and hope never to see again. I also have never gotten over that face in the sky, the face of Günther Gotthold Hanns. He was looking down at D.C. Austerlitz as if angry with him about something. I'm not exactly sure if that was it, because his appearance was so brief, but it was his face, that I know."

Some people in Nuremberg dismissed this as hearsay and said Wolf V. Haassenkamp was just seeking attention. But many believed him and said it was a sign that Günther Gotthold Hanns did not want anyone using the original recipe as a way to make money for selfish reasons, and cursed anyone who did, because the bakery that once belonged to him was also burned down. There were no witnesses on sight when that happened, but the devastation was identical to what had taken place in D.C. Austerlitz's field.

The ginger cookie empire, its recipe and its owner were gone. Since D.C. Austerlitz was the only one with the recipe — because he feared his staff would run off with the recipe and set up their own shops — no one else had it. The original ingredients could be used no more. This brought an end to the original taste of the gingerbread cookie.

∾

Declan flipped to the final pages of the book and saw pictures of two people on one page titled "Founders and Contributors to the Man of Ginger Cookie." Underneath each picture were their names. "Oh my gosh," Declan murmured, "she looks like a man!"

❧ Christina's Secret

Declan and Layla met at the Cherryfield Community Park, just minutes away from Christina Liu's home. Declan noted from the research Layla had come up with that she was a busy one. She had weekly piano and swimming lessons, and was a member of the Children's Orchestra Society of Cherryfield and a volunteer at both the Zhao Tang Chinese Museum and the Cherryfield Gingerbread Association. And he thought *he* was busy.

"Ambitious, isn't she?" Layla said as Declan re-read Christina's information. "Could you imagine the kind of press coverage she would get if she baked gingerbread cookies for the Gingerbread Association using G.G. Nana's recipe? CCB Television and

The Cherryfield Times would be right at her doorstep waiting to interview her. She would tell them about the associations she belongs to, the lessons she takes, and boom, become an instant star," Layla mocked.

According to Layla's research, some of the people closest to Christina mentioned her determination to become a famous pianist. According to two members of the Orchestra Society of Cherryfield, Christina had gone out of her way to make sure she had at least one solo performance, even though the purpose of the society was to perform as a group. They said she rarely mingled with other members during or after rehearsal and remained completely focused on delivering flawless performances.

"Yeah, G.G. Nana's recipe would certainly give her fame, a whole bunch of it." Declan turned his attention to Layla. "And she would most likely be appointed chairperson of the Cherryfield Gingerbread Association for Children, and knock Zoie completely out of the picture. As my grandfather says, ambition knows no evil."

"Ambition knows no *boundaries*, not evil!" Layla corrected.

"Whatever." Declan put his notes and steno pad into his knapsack. "All I know is that someone with her ambition might do anything.

This is not going to be an easy interrogation, I can feel it."

❧

In the living room, Declan and Layla found Christina sitting in front of a black baby grand piano playing music by Wolfgang Amadeus Mozart. Declan knew the composer only because he'd been forced to watch a performance by Shining Rays of Light at Operetta City Music Centre during a grade four school trip.

"Hi, Christina," Layla said. "Sorry for interrupting. Your mother said we could come in."

Christina almost jolted out of her seat. She then quickly turned her head in their direction, swinging her long, straight black ponytail in the opposite direction. "Oh, Layla, Declan, what a pleasant surprise," she finally responded. "An extremely pleasant surprise." She got up off the piano bench to greet them with a lovely smile plastered on her face, which only seconds ago had worn a scowl. "I need a break anyway."

"That was great! Are you practicing for a recital?" Layla asked.

"Yes, I have one coming up for Christmas. It's called *Noel*."

"How do you do it? I mean you belong to so many associations, take piano and swimming

53

lessons, and on top of that you have school and homework. I find it tough enough just taking swimming and yoga lessons and being a committee member for the Keep Cherryfield Clean Association. Can you offer me some tips?" Layla asked, sounding completely sincere.

"It's all a matter of how you manage your time," a blushing Christina answered, waving a hand in the air as if it was that simple.

As Christina provided tips on time management, Declan decide to learn a bit more about the suspect.

He walked over to the mantel and found three red-framed pictures. One was of a man with short black hair who strongly resembled Christina, standing behind a seated woman with the same hair colour that reached her jaw line. There was a little boy sitting on her lap. Standing on either side were a boy of about seven and Christina, wearing a purple bubble dress with her black hair down.

The picture on the other end of the mantel was of an elderly woman with black and a few grey hairs tied up in a bun. She sat with her hands folded in her lap. Sitting beside her was a man of a similar age wearing, what was that Declan wondered as he squinted his eyes and moved closer to get a better view, a golden fortune cookie pendant. *Okay then*, he thought, *whatever*.

But the most interesting picture was that of a pig-tailed Christina sitting on the lap of none other than the gingerbread man himself. They both stared into his eyes, showing every tooth. In the bottom corner of the photograph was signed, "To my favourite gingerbread helper. The Gingerbread Man. XXXX."

What would the gingerbread man's favourite volunteer do to keep being his favourite? Well, Declan was about to find out. But just as he was about to open his mouth, he noticed a mini photo album sitting on a mahogany end table. On the cover it said, "Though the Years – Christina and the Gingerbread Man." Just below that there was a picture of the gingerbread man cradling an infant. Flipping through the pictures, Declan noticed another photo of Christina with the gingerbread man one year older then the last.

"... so as I said, Layla, it's not..."

"I see you and the gingerbread man are very good friends," Declan interrupted, holding up the photo album.

Shocked, Christina quickly snatched the album out of his hand. "Haven't your parents ever taught you not to snoop through other people's things?"

"Yes, they did. And when I'm not working, I don't. Christina, do you know anything about Samantha's missing gingerbread penguin?"

She paused for a second, as if thinking of what to say. "Um, well yes, I know of its disappearance, Javier mentioned it a few days ago. What about it?"

"Well, as you may or may not know, Samantha hired us to find it. Since you were at her place on the evening it went missing, we thought you might be a good person to help us locate it," Declan answered.

"I don't know how I could do that, since I don't know who stole it," she answered in a snooty tone.

"Do these look familiar to you?" Declan pulled out the same Post-it notes he'd shown Javier and Addison.

"No, they don't!" Her response was immediate.

"How do you know that?" He studied her. "You haven't even read them."

"Well, I don't use those to write on."

"I never said you did." He put them back in the envelope. "When was the last time you saw the gingerbread penguin?"

"Ah, that would have to be when Samantha's nana came into the entertainment room and asked her to take the cookie to her room."

"But how did you know she returned it to her bedroom?" Declan asked.

"She told us. How else would I know?"

"She said she didn't mention where it would be placed. She said it was usually kept in her parents' room, because of the diamonds. It was only at the last second she decided to put it in her room. I just spoke with her a few days about this. So really, how did you know?"

"Ah, well...I guess Javier told me." Christina averted her eyes.

"Oh, so I guess that means Javier stole the cookie," Layla added. "I mean how else would he know where the cookie was if she didn't mention it to any of you?"

"He didn't steal that cookie, I know he didn't."

"Is that because you know who did?" Layla enquired.

Christina paused for a second then laughed. "Are you implying that I stole the cookie? How could I carry that hippo cookie to the front door without dropping it, let alone carry it home?"

"You and Samantha are about the same height and size," Layla pointed out. "If she can carry it, so can you."

"Well, I didn't take it home or anywhere else. And why would I? Why would I need a cursed cookie?" she asked with more than a trace of irritation.

"Oh, let's see." Layla put a finger to the corner of her mouth then turned her eyes to the ceiling as she feigned needing time to think. "Oh, I got one for you, your grandfather's grocery store, what's the name of it again? Yes,

Liu's Fresh Fruits and Vegetables. I hear it has a competitor, Fresh Harvest and Groceries. They opened up just a few blocks away from your granddad's store. My mom said the prices are much cheaper and the food is just as fresh. Plus you can get all your groceries at one place, whereas you can't do that at your grandfather's store."

"My grandfather's business is doing just fine," Christina retorted, clearly offended. "But even if it wasn't, what would that have to do with me and the missing cookie?"

"Much." Layla got straight to the point. "Cheaper prices would mean your grandfather's number one customer, the Cherryfield Gingerbread Association, would give its business to this new grocery store and not your grandfather's. I learned through my sources that this is starting to happen. But if you were to come up with delicious recipe that would help the association increase the money they make, they would feel obligated to continue buying ginger roots from your grandfather."

Christina couldn't find an intelligent response to the picture Layla had just painted. "That's crazy!"

"I think so too. But you know I'm right."

Christina walked away from them and sat back on the piano bench. She stayed silent for a few seconds. Then turning to face them, she opened her mouth as if she was about to say something, maybe even confess something. Just as she was about to speak, she stopped herself. She closed her eyes and then stared at her hands in her lap. Her near admission frustrated Declan.

"Okay, Christina, here's a reason I'm sure you won't think is so crazy. You and Zoie are running a bitter campaign against one another to become chairperson of the Cherryfield Gingerbread Association's children's division. It's well known that the two of you hate one another and this campaign is less about becoming chairperson and more about winning."

"Is not," Christina scowled.

"But what is not known," Declan continued as if she'd said nothing, "well, at least not until now, is that you are trailing Zoie by 37 points according to a recent survey conducted by the Cherryfield Gingerbread Association. With only four weeks to go until Election Day, your team has been begging you to withdraw. But I think your hate for Zoie has blinded you, and you will do anything to stop her from winning, so you don't look bad, look like a loser."

"That is not true!" Christina shot up off of her seat. "I didn't start this war with Zoie, she did!" she squealed.

"Maybe so, but wouldn't you agree that coming up with a unique recipe like G.G. Nana's and winning the chairperson's seat is a great way to get back at her for everything she's done to you since you were little?"

"I will win this election, you watch and see. And I will do it without spreading vicious lies, and buying votes with cookies and baked goods, doing homework for free, and I will do this without G.G. Nana's stinking recipe. I will win this with honesty and hard work. On November 16, Zoie will be just a horrible nightmare." Christina was almost in a frenzy.

"Well, I hope..."

"Unlike Zoie," Christina continued, "I don't have the time to suck up to members and volunteers of the Gingerbread Association and act like I'm miss perfect with pretty little gingerbread muffins and houses. I'm too busy! I have a life. I can't be all things to all people. I can't do everything! I n-e-e-d a break! Oh gosh," she cupped her face with both hands as if surprised by her outburst. "How could I have..." and then immediately stopped herself mid-sentence.

Declan and Layla could only stare at her unravelling. For the first time Declan realized that Christina was not super kid after all. She was just like the rest of them. Feeling the urge to comfort her, he walked to her and patted her on her shoulder, "I know what it's like to be busy. It can be so tiring sometimes. And sometimes when we feel that we can only do so much, we might feel desperate to find a way to make things easier. No one's blaming you for that, Christina. I can see you're under a lot of pressure. But it still doesn't make it right to steal. Give it back to us now and we won't mention a word of this to anyone."

He could feel Christina taking a deep breath as her shoulder rose up. She closed her eyes, almost as if saying a prayer. When she opened them, she looked Declan dead in the eyes. "GET OUT!" She pointed to the door. Declan almost jumped out of his skin. "I said get out! Now! I'm never going to speak with the two of you again, never!" she shouted.

Declan walked away with numb ears and gathered his knapsack. "For your sake, I hope you never have to. But if we find out you have the cookie, you'll have no choice but to speak with us. Don't practice too hard!"

"Arghhhh!" Christina grunted.

"Oh, by the way, beautiful piano," Layla said admiringly, just before the front door shut.

"Whew!" She blew air out of her slightly parted lips as she zipped up her vest. "Well, that went just great!"

"At least we got out of there alive." Declan shook his head as he looked back at the two-storey beige house. "Boy, she really scares me sometimes. So what did you think about what just happened in there?"

"She seemed nervous, jittery. There were a couple of times when she seemed as if she was about to tell us something, but then changed her mind."

"I thought the same thing," Declan agreed. "She may have wanted to confess about taking the cookie, but was afraid doing so would cost her Samantha's friendship."

"But you told her we wouldn't mention it to anyone if she handed the cookie over to us. So that can't be the reason why."

"I don't know." Declan watched all seventeen pounds of Pumpkin, the Millar's cat, play with a yellow rubber ball on the lawn. "But she's definitely hiding something. Boy, she was so close to confessing. How difficult could it be to just say, I stole the cookie! Boom and it's over! No more worries, no more secrets, life goes on."

"It's easy for us to say, we didn't steal the cookie."

"Yeah, I know," Declan said. "That's why we were hired, because confessions only come with proof of evidence. And right now we are as close to that as we were when we started this case."

"Declan, you sound as if you doubt we'll solve this one."

"We have no confessions, no clues. We just have three suspects with very good motives, and no evidence to back it up." Declan frowned. "Why shouldn't I doubt we'll solve this case?"

"Declan, I have to admit, this isn't an easy case to solve. You can't expect us to have all the answers in a few days."

"Layla, we've been working on this case for two weeks and we have less then two weeks to solve it before the gala. It not being an easy case to solve just isn't good enough." Declan said as they stood on Layla's walkway.

Layla took a deep breath. "You know what I think we should do when we go home? Work on anything but this case. Just for tonight," she said, when he was about to argue. "You've got a book review due for your next meeting with Inspire Children to Read, and I've got a report to write up on Eradicating Bubble Gum in Public Places for my next meeting with the Keep Cherryfield Clean Association. This is becoming a serious problem in our community, and it has to stop before our streets and sidewalks are covered with bubble gum," she added heatedly. "Anyway, I think this will give us a break from this case, and then we can get together tomorrow to go over everything we've gathered with a fresh focus." When he said nothing, she prodded him. "Okay?"

"Okay," he finally said.

"Oh, Declan, have you decided what costume you're going to wear for the Blake's Halloween Party?"

"I'm deciding on two, but I want to keep it as a surprise until the party." His anxiety over the case was briefly replaced with excitement for the upcoming party. "I wish we could have them every week."

"That would be sweet! Well, since you won't tell me what you're wearing, I won't tell you what Nigel and I are wearing. Yes," she said with a victorious smile when he gave her a surprised look, "I know what Nigel is wearing, but I didn't find out from him. Anyway, we only have five more days to go, see you tomorrow!"

❧ The Threat

Layla was right. He needed a break from this case, Declan tried to convince himself. It would only be for tonight and then they would be right back at it tomorrow. He needed this time to work on his book review of *Lester the Polar Bear: His Life in Jamaica.*

He flicked on the light switch in his agency, walked over to his desk and stuffed the book in his knapsack. As he was leaving, he noticed something on the floor next to the entrance. Declan froze. It was an envelope with the words, I AM WATCHING YOU SNOOPY INVESTIGATOR typed on it. He grabbed it, tore it open, pulled the letter out, then read the typed note:

You will not solve this case. Want to know why?? Because you're stupid and I am smart! And if you care about your bushy hair friend's bones you will stop the investagation on the gingerbread penguin now. Because if you don't Layla will have a very bad acident.

Singed

Eyes watching you

A grip of fear came over Declan as he stared into the eyes on the letter. For a few seconds they seemed almost as real as the letter in his hand. Well, at least there were only two spelling errors on this one. The wonders of spell check.

This kid was disturbed. Not only was this person obsessed, but violent. He had never worked on a case where he dealt with a violent person. And he guessed he never would, because he couldn't continue to work on this case and put Layla at risk. No, that was out of the question.

He walked back to his desk and sat down to read the letter again and again and again. Nothing! Absolutely nothing in it gave even a hint of who wrote it. Whoever wrote this was right about one thing, they were smart.

Threatening his best friend's safety was a sure way to get him to drop this case.

It bothered him that someone else was calling the shots, telling him what to do, controlling him like a puppeteer controls a puppet. If it were his life in danger, there was no way he would have stopped. In truth, it would have been fuel to dig deeper into the investigation and solve the case.

He'd call Samantha first thing in the morning to let her know he was dropping the case, he decided as he slipped the letter back into the envelope. Layla would be stopping by tomorrow, so he'd have to make up some excuse why he couldn't continue working on it. He couldn't think of a good lie at the moment, but he'd deal with that tomorrow. Right now, he had to clean up for dinner and then start his book review. He looked around his desk, gathered what he needed and walked to the door. "Bejeebers!" he said out loud, with a trace of anger. He didn't want to give it up. What he wanted was to nail the punk more than ever. "But I guess that won't be happening." He slammed the door.

❧

Declan dreamed of Halloween, haunted houses, opaque ghosts and a trail of bones in a graveyard with Layla's head as a tombstone. He sprang out of his sleep in a cold sweat.

Sitting up straight as an arrow on his bed, he looked around his bedroom to make sure it was just that. When the room came into focus, he turned on his lamp to help shake off the fear, and wiped the sweat from his forehead with his hand. The gingerbread thief was even threatening his dreams.

It was 3:52 a.m., he saw as he glanced at his clock next to his lamp. Oh boy was he tired. He yawned, but too spooked to go back to sleep. So he got out of bed and went to his work desk. Staring out into the night, he could see the full moon. He logged onto his computer and reached for his knapsack sitting next to his desk. *This should help keep me awake,* he thought as he put the book he'd been reviewing on his desk. He'd been so distracted earlier by that letter that he couldn't concentrate on what to write. Now he wanted nothing more than to be distracted. He only hoped his parents didn't hear him as he started to type.

🦢 Recipe Time My Friend

Something was bugging Declan about this. He yawned while examining the letter for the 30th time. He just couldn't put his finger on it.

He'd tried to reach Samantha earlier this morning, but her father said she was shopping with her mom and would not be back until the afternoon. So he made an attempt to busy himself with homework while waiting for her call. It was pointless. His concentration was shot. "Shouldn't she be back by now?" He reached for the receiver to call her again.

He heard a knock and then saw the door open. It was Samantha. "Hi, Declan," she said apologetically. "I'm, ah, sorry for stopping by unexpectedly, but I have something you really need to see."

"Ah...Samantha, listen. There's something I've got to tell you." Declan straightened in his chair as he struggled to think of an intelligent lie to tell her. It would have been so much easier by phone, he thought. "I don't know quite how to say this, but I can't work on this case any more. I'm sorry, but um...I've been taking on too many cases lately and it's...ah, beginning to affect the time I spend on my homework. Sorry." He averted his eyes.

"What?" Samantha sounded dumbfounded. "But Declan, you can't do that! You promised me that you would do your best to find the cookie. The gala is in less than two weeks."

"Samantha, maybe you should tell your parents about what happened. I'm sure they would h..."

"I can't do that!" She shook her head. "I've kept it from them for too long. They would never trust me with anything ever again."

"How do you know that? I mean, has anything like this ever happened to you before?" She shook her head. "Then I think you should give it a try. They probably will come up with more than I have." *Which is nothing,* he said to himself as he yawned. "I could even give you all the research I've gathered." He started gathering some lose sheets of paper on his desk and put them into a pile. He opened a drawer and pulled out a folder titled, "Kidnapped

Gingerbread Penguin." *I do not want to give this case up, I do not want to give this case up, I do not want to give this case up, he kept saying to himself,* almost like an affirmation. "It's not much, but it's a start." He handed them to her.

She didn't reach for them. Her eyes started to water. "Why can't you dump one of your other cases? Why mine? Why are you doing this to me, Declan?" A tear dropped to her cheek as her voice started to tremble. "What is it, am I not paying you enough? If that's the reason," she went on just as Declan was about to say something, "then I can make weekly payments from my allowance, just name your price. But not too much please, I only get..."

"I don't want more money, Samantha." Declan was exhausted at her persistence. Why couldn't she just leave this alone? "I can't do it. I just can't do it all." He thought back to that moving speech Christina had made yesterday. "It's not because I don't want to, Samantha, but..."

"But," Layla said, standing in the doorway with her hands on her hips. "Please, Declan, don't let me stop you, as you were saying."

"He said he has too many cases that he's working on and that they're interfering with his school work, so he has no choice but to drop my case, *mine!*" Samantha got out of her seat.

"Really, Declan." Layla raised an eyebrow. "We, you and me," she pointed to herself, "have too many cases on our hands?"

Declan's face turned lobster red. He looked down at his desk to avoid her glare, only partially taking in the clutter on his desk, as he tried to wiggle his way out of this mess. "Layla, this is my investigation firm. I decide how many cases we work on and that's final. I'm sorry Samantha, but I'm afraid you're going to have to find someone else to help you solve..."

"*Your* firm!" Layla bellowed. "I've been with *your* firm almost from the beginning. It was with *my* help that you solved most of *our* cases." She ranted on. "I'm glad to finally learn this is what you think of me, as a second fiddle and not a partner. And to think you're my best friend." Declan could see the hurt on her face, but what choice did he have in the matter? "Well, if this is what you think of me, I quit!"

"Layla, no, you can't do that! You're overreacting."

"Oh, no you didn't! So now you think you can tell me what to do, huh?"

"No, no! I wasn't trying to...Layla, you got this all wrong. Of course I don't see you as a second fiddle." He spoke coolly, hoping it would help to calm her down. "You're right, I wouldn't be able to do this without you. I need you. That's why I don't want you to go, and you're my best friend.

But I can't work on Samantha's case any more. Please trust me on this, as my best friend."

"How can I trust you if you won't tell me what's going on?" She walked a couple of steps closer to him. "We're best friends, we're partners. You've always told me everything."

He could see how upset she was. *Oh, this is not fair.* He only wished he could tell her, but he knew what her reaction would be. It would be exactly like his. She would want to solve the case even more. "I'm sorry, Layla, I can't tell you. It's for the best."

She wasn't happy with his response. "Okay, fine," she said icily then turned to Samantha. "Samantha, I have the time to continue working on your case, and since I no longer work for Declan, I would like to continue working on it, if you'll let me."

Panic choked him. "No, Layla, you can't work on this case. Listen to me."

"I'm done listening to you, Declan."

"That's right, Layla, don't listen to him," Samantha said. "Of course you can work on my case! Thank you! I owe you." She hugged Layla. "Let's go to my place so we can talk about..."

"Enough!" Declan wailed, raising his hands in the air. "Fine. If you continue to work on this case, you may end up seriously injured. Not by me," he added when he saw her eyes widen in horror, "but by...here, see for yourself."

He reached for the letter and envelope he'd tucked into his drawer when Samantha came in, handed it to her and then paced back and forth while the girls read it.

"Oh, this is serious, Layla." Samantha placed a hand to her mouth and then turned to Declan. "Declan, I think you're right. I'm going to speak with my parents about this. Layla, I would never be able to live with myself if anything happened to you. I can't ask you to take that kind of risk for me."

"No, you won't, Samantha." Layla put a hand on Samantha's shoulder. "I know what you are trying to do, both of you." She looked at Declan. "And I appreciate it. But I don't need any protecting from this bully. There's no way this," she raised the letter, "is going to scare me from solving this case. When we catch whoever did this, they will wish they never sent it."

"This is exactly why I didn't tell you. I knew you would respond this way." Declan yawned. "Layla, listen to Samantha and me, this kid is a sicko. The recipe obviously means more to this person than any of us could have ever imagined. I mean, to threaten bodily harm to someone says a lot. We can't work on this case anymore. You can't work on it alone. Forget it!"

"Declan, we can't stop working on this case now. We've spent too much time on it. Plus if we stop working on it because of a threat, then we'll stop working on the next one because of a threat and so on. And if that happens, there would be no point in having an investigative agency. If we quit now, whoever kidnapped the cookie wins. We can't let that happen."

Declan could not open his mouth. Layla was right. There was no point in having an agency if you chickened out of a case because of threats, regardless of who it was directed at. He had never faced a situation like this before. The only thing he could think of was Layla's safety.

"I'm not going to let you give up this case," Layla continued. "And if you do, I'll work on it myself without your help or Samantha's permission. I will not let this kid tell me what to do." She folded her arms on her chest defiantly. "So what's it going to be, partner, Samantha?"

Samantha and Declan looked at each other as if defeated. Samantha shrugged. "I'd rather you not, but if you're going to do it anyway, then you have my support."

"And you?" Layla asked Declan.

She'd outsmarted him, he realized. What more could he say or do. "Well, since I can't stop you, I guess I have no other choice but to stay on the case. But you can't go anywhere without Nigel or myself, except to the girls' washroom, of course."

"Yaaaaaaaay!" Layla jumped up and down with a smug smile. "Great! So now can we talk about this case and nail the fear monger?"

"Actually, I'd like to show you both something," Samantha interrupted. She went into her turquoise corduroy bucket purse with pink pom-poms on the side, pulled out an envelope and handed it to Declan. Layla moved next to him to read it as well.

RECIPE TIME MY FRIEND was typed on the envelope. Declan noticed the font size and envelope was identical to the one he received yesterday. He pulled the letter from the already torn-open envelope and began to read it.

Our friendship is forever and ever and ever. That's why it is only right that you give me the receipe. We're friends. We are suppose to share everything.

Here is what I want you to do, place the exact receipe in an envelope and mark it "Yours to keep" then place it in a book called "Master in the Kitchen" at the Cherryfield Public Library at 4:00 p.m. sharp this Tuesday.

I will make the gingerbread cookie using this receipe on Wednesday. If it taste exactly like your G.G. Nana's, I will leave you a letter telling you where and when you can pick up the gingerbread penguin, if it doesn't, I will crush your huge cookie into crumbs and mix it with the sand at Rush Side Beach.

Remember, I don't want to hurt the cookie, so if I do, it will be your fault.

Singed,
Friend forever

"When did you get this?" Layla asked.

"I'm pretty sure it was Friday. I didn't bother to do any homework that day, so I didn't go into my knapsack until yesterday. That's when I found it. I assumed someone slipped it in there at school when I was distracted."

"You mean one of your closest friends," Declan added. "That's if we are to go by what the letter says, which I am." He shook his head as he scanned the letter again. Like the one he'd received, there was something strange about this one. He just could not figure out what it was.

"It's starting to look that way." Samantha appeared saddened by the revelation.

Declan and Layla exchanged glances. "Samantha, do you plan to give the ingredients of the original recipe this Tuesday?" Declan asked.

"What choice do I have?"

"I don't know," Declan answered. "I wish there was another way around it." He paused for a few seconds. "Well, whatever you decide, make sure to let us know and tell no one else. This is very important. Layla, Nigel and I will be at the library working on our history project that day. We'll make sure to keep our eyes and ears open to see just who stops by to pick up 'Master in the Kitchen.'" Declan yawned and sat back down at his desk. "Is it okay if I keep this?" He pointed to the letter. Samantha nodded.

"Declan, I don't think I've ever seen you yawn so much. What's up?" Layla asked.

"I've had a very late night." Declan planted an elbow on his desk then rested his chin in the cup of his hand. "Samantha, one more request — would you go over everything that happened on the day the gingerbread penguin disappeared from beginning to end? I just want to make sure we're not overlooking anything."

The Witness Who Knows Nothing and Everything

"Whoever pulled this off is a genius," Declan pointed out as he paced the agency floor, just seconds after Samantha left. "I mean, you have a house full of people, and yet someone managed to get that huge cookie out of it and take it to whatever hiding place it's at without anyone noticing. It's like magic without a magician."

"Samantha did mention that they all had knapsacks," Layla said, reading her notes on the case.

"Yeah, I know, but that cookie is too big to fit entirely into any of their knapsacks. There has to be another way it got out of the house."

"Maybe they didn't put it in anything at first. Maybe they took the cookie and placed it in the garden between the flowers and then went back for it when they believed it was safe to do so," Layla suggested. "Samantha did say they all left at different times."

"And risk the chance of it getting trampled on by a stray animal, or even worse, a kid trying to catch a flying Frisbee," Declan said doubt-fully. "Whoever did this is too smart to take a chance like that."

"They could all be in this together," Layla said. "They were alone while Samantha left the entertainment room. Maybe they decided to leave separately so they could get something large enough to put in it and then somehow get it to the one who stayed behind. That person would then hand it to them and it's gone."

"Yeah, that crossed my mind, too," Declan agreed. "But the only problem with that is they wouldn't get full credit for its discovery. And eventually, people would find out the recipe from all of them, or their family members are the same." He raked his hand through his already dishevelled hair. "Layla, we've reached a dead end on this one."

"Declan, let's go through what happened that day from the time they went in the back-yard to play Zooloretto, step-by-step." She got her pencil and turned to a blank page in her steno notebook to write down the points, refus-ing to admit defeat. "They each took turns going to the washroom or wherever."

"None of this proves…"

Layla sighed. "Declan, I'm not finished. Let's try to work through this. Nothing else is working, so we have nothing to lose. Samantha told us Addison went to the washroom first, then Javier and lastly Christina.

"Addison confessed to going in Samantha's bedroom, so if he took it, and Javier and Christina went in there later, then they know it went missing once we told them Samantha put it in her bedroom. Christina could suspect that either Javier or Addison stole it, if she went in there, because they both left the patio before her.

"If Javier went into the bedroom and saw the cookie there, then that would clear Addison of taking it, but not Javier and Christina. Declan, we need to find out if Javier and Christina went into Samantha's bedroom," she said bluntly.

Declan started to feel a little more energized from Layla's analysis. "If Javier and Christina both admit they were in Samantha's bedroom and saw the cookie that would mean Christina took it, since both Addison and Javier had left by then. I think she knows an admission like that would be as good as saying she kidnapped the cookie."

"Well, it could be possible that one of them took it when they left."

"No, it's not. Remember Samantha said her mom escorted each of them to the door so she could lock it." Declan leaned against his desk.

"You're right." Layla put her pencil and steno pad on Declan's desk. "Well, maybe she noticed the bulkiness of their knapsacks."

"I don't think Mrs. Tate takes notice of things like that."

"Declan you're being difficult." She frowned. "You're fighting me on every theory I've given you, and I'm getting a headache because of it."

"Sorry for the headache."

"I think we need a break right now. I'm sure we'll find out when we go to the library on Tuesday who's behind this. Let's go to the park. We told Nigel we'd be there at three."

"Not right now," he said curtly. "Maybe I'll catch up with you guys later."

"Declan, you're obsessing over this case. You really need a break from it." She sounded concerned.

"I'm not obsessed. I'm just doing what I was hired to do." He knew he sounded rude, but there was not much he could do about it at the moment, given the mood he was in. "Just go to the park with Nigel."

"You said I shouldn't go anywhere without you," Layla taunted.

"Layla, I just got the letter yesterday. The kidnapper doesn't know what I've decided yet."

"Fine, be a sucky baby! I'm going. If you see any broken bones..."

"Layla, stop it! Just remember, you were the one who insisted we continue to work on this case, so leave me alone."

"I will." Layla walked to the door. "Hope you come by later. We'll be there until five thirty." The door shut.

I didn't think she'd ever leave, Declan said to himself. Layla was a great partner. But after receiving that letter, getting so little sleep last night and having so few clues on this case – correction, no clues, he needed to be alone so he could have some time to think about everything going on in his head. And there was a lot going on at the moment, especially after his conversation with her.

He sifted through the pile of papers on his desk for his notebook and started to write down some of those thoughts. There was nothing new coming up. He read over the points and closed the notebook in frustration. *Not one clue, not one,* he thought while absently scanning his desk. He had never worked on a case where he didn't have at least one clue at this stage of the investigation. His attention then focused on the folder he had offered Samantha earlier. He reached for it and started to read through the first few pages that came at him, the ones Layla had taken when they questioned each suspect. She had typed them out for him so they would be easier to read. It was pointless going over these again, he knew, but what else did he have to do other than homework?

Reading through the pages, Declan noticed one thing, it wasn't pointless. Not this time. Why hadn't he noticed this earlier? "It's so obvious!" he said. It was staring him right in the face, and he hadn't even seen it. Could this be the clue that solves the case? He thought with hope growing inside of him. Well, he would most certainly find out.

Layla was right: they needed to speak with Addison, Javier and Christina again and, as an afterthought, Mrs. Tate. Yes! That's right. She might know more about this without even knowing it. Feeling less tired and more energized than he had all day, Declan put the two letters into the folder and then stuffed it into his knapsack along with his notebook. He'd have to be careful how he went about questioning her. He didn't want her knowing he was hired by Samantha to recover the gingerbread penguin.

He'd also have to speak with Samantha again. He hadn't questioned her about who was with her yesterday when that envelope was stuffed into her knapsack.

Oh, he was feeling good about this. *About time,* he thought as he slipped into his bomber jacket. This could be the breakthrough they were looking for.

Boo! Its Halloween

Walking through the Blake's lawn felt like walking through a cemetery, Declan thought, and with good reason. The yellowish green grass on the lawn was full of cobweb-covered tombstones. Many of them had the letters "R.I.P." on them. There were fluorescent decapitated limbs that changed colours, skeleton bones scattered around them and a coffin resting diagonally on three inches of the Blake's walkway with a pair of human hands trying to claw its way out. About two feet away on the opposite side of the walkway was a pair of hands coming out from the ground holding a sign that read, "ENTER IF YOU DARE, BUT YOU MIGHT NOT EXIT!" Beside this was a witch that appeared to be a thousand years old. She was holding a shiny apple in one hand, offering it to anyone who would take it and a small cauldron in the other.

There were bats with neon amber eyes that flashed on and off hanging from tree branches, along with a single grim reaper dressed in a dull grey torn cloth, an apparition of a man carrying a snake walking towards them. He stopped and then repeated this same ritual again and again. And a tune sung in a creepy voice played outside the house demanding the head of Frankenstein and begging listeners to scream if they must, intensifying the feeling of death and doom.

Approaching the entrance, Declan noticed the giant face of a black cat and a sinister green creature looking out of the windows. Each of them had an eerie glow coming from their eyes.

Standing on each side of the doorway, mummies greeted Declan and Layla. They had caved in eyes, protruding cheekbones and large teeth. "Good evening! You're looking smashing as usual. Make sure not to get any blood on that outfit of yours. Hahahahahaha!"

"AHHHHHHHHHHH!!!" Layla screamed.

Declan almost jumped out of his skin at the unexpected sounds. He looked down in the direction where the baritone voice had come from and saw a dwarf size zombie standing next to the mummy on Layla's side. It was holding its cut-off head in its hands.

"Oh my goodness, Declan, these Halloween props have got me so spooked! They look and seem so real," Layla panted, getting back her bearings after the fright.

"You're telling me." Declan looked around to make sure there were no more unexpected surprises waiting for them. "I feel like I've entered the world of the living dead. Now, Layla, you remember what you're supposed to do and when you are to do it, right?"

"Of course I do!" She rolled her eyes and sighed.

"Okay, just checking. I don't want to mess this up and possibly endanger the life of the cookie." He rang the doorbell.

"Good evening!" A doorman dressed as a box of Kleenex greeted them. "Please, allow me to take your coats, mademoiselle, monsieur. Ah-choo!" he sneezed. "Excuse me," he apologized then went off.

"Well, at least he has lots of tissue," Declan whispered. They both laughed.

Declan adjusted his cape and the sword in the sheath of his gladiator custom. He almost refused to take off his coat, he was so cold. *Why is it that every Halloween is the coldest day in October*? he wondered.

Layla seemed to be as cold as him. She was shivering in her 1970s-inspired psyche-delic hippie dress and matching huge earrings shaped like the letter O, yellow leather visor hat and boots. Her normally ringlet afro was straightened, falling several inches below her shoulders.

"Well, look who it is." Layla's teeth clattered as she looked at the kidnapper laughing away with a group of kids in the party room.

"Who would have... Wow, Layla, would you look at this!" Declan lost track of what he was about to say when he spotted a life-size Pez dispenser standing at the entrance of the ballroom. It had a clown face and a pair of hands wrapped in black gloves. The dispenser itself was blue and had what appeared to be a vending machine filled with normal size Pez dispensers in it.

Declan reached to pull one out. S-L-A-P! "Don't touch me, you fool!" the Pez dispenser lashed out in a foreign accent after slapping Declan's hand.

"Ouch!" Declan rubbed his stinging hand as he examined the dispenser to see if it was human. "Fine, keep your stupid Pez dispensers!"

"Declan, are you okay?" Layla looked at his hand and then the life-size dispenser.

"Yeah, I'm fine," Declan responded, still inspecting the dispenser. "Come on, let's go inside and eat."

❧

At the buffet table, Declan piled his plate with as much sweets as he could get on it. He loved sweets. If he had it his way, they would be the only things he'd ever eat. Javier was really lucky to have a father who could bake like this.

He put down his plate so he could pour blood-red punch into a skull cup with the ladle sitting in a skull bowl.

Every Halloween, a family in the community has a party for the kids. This party was by far the coolest one yet, Declan thought as he scanned the ballroom. The decorations inside the house were as impressive as the ones outside, but not nearly as terrifying. The walls and some furniture were decorated with cobwebs. Tattered black cloths covered the tables with plastic spiders scattered on top. On one of the tables, sitting in a corner of the room, were candles of pumpkins and skull heads, black crows, a cauldron and a mirror. In another corner, five life-size skeletons sat at a dinette table eating a meal. Sitting in the centre of the table was a crystal ball with a witch in it as a fortune teller. On the floor next to them were two wild black cats and a witch's broom that leaned against the wall.

The ceiling had black twig garlands from which hung feathered bats, and a trio of tarantulas crawled up the stair railing. Just below the stairs sat a family of carved pumpkins of various sizes clustered together with light emanating from them.

Most of the guests were kids from his school. They were all wearing costumes, some cool, others out-of-this-world weird. A cool costume wearer came to greet him – it was Moo Moo the dog. She was wearing a royal blue police officer's uniform with all the equipment no good officer would leave a police station without. She had handcuffs, a walkie-talkie and even a police hat.

She barked at him as she jogged towards him. She was asking him to pet her, Declan knew. "Hey cutie." He crouched down and brushed what little of her body was not covered in police garb. "How ya doing? Hope you're not getting into anymore ice cream parlours and making yourself sick."

She whimpered.

"Oops! Sorry." He tried to soothe her. "Shouldn't have mentioned that." Declan then looked over at the kidnapper. "You know, maybe I could use your help." He used one of his hands to cup Moo Moo's face. "That might take your mind off of you–know-what."

"Hey, Declan!" Sable greeted Declan. She was dressed as Cleopatra. Her long hair was pulled back off her face and topped with a gold sequined head piece. "Where are Layla and Nigel?

Declan stood up. "Oh, Layla's around here somewhere. And Nigel was forced to go to his cousin's Halloween party. I feel sorry for him. He really wanted to come with us."

"Oh!" She sounded disappointed. "Well, I'm going to go get something to drink. See you later."

Declan scanned the room looking for Layla and spotted her in deep conversation with Pradeep. Correction, Pardeep was in deep conversation with Layla. She looked as if she was trying to find an opening to escape.

"Layla, I've been looking all over the place for you! Where have you been?"

"Well, I was just talking..."

"Never mind." He deliberately cut her off. "Come on, we haven't even eaten yet." He said carry an entire plate of food in his hand.

"But Layla, I wasn't finished explaining why I disagree with your report on Eradicating Bubble Gum in Public Places," Pardeep pointed out. He was wearing an orange astronaut suit and transparent gold and white helmet.

"That's okay! I forgive you," she shouted back to him. "Oh, thank you, Declan, for that." She seemed relieved. "He never lets up on these things. I've been trying to get away from him for the past fifteen minutes. Anyway, how is our perpetrator doing?" She grabbed a plate and started piling it up with sweets.

"If I didn't know what I know, I would have never guessed it. It's as if everything's normal." He plopped a white eyeball truffle into his mouth.

"Well, soon everything will be out in the open. I just hope we're able to get the cookie back to Samantha in one piece." Layla added a pumpkin-shaped ghoul cheese sandwich and spooky eyeball tacos to her mix of sweets. "It's too bad we couldn't nail the thief at the library."

"This kid is very clever. Getting someone else to sign the book out the next day when we were all in school was perfect. Always one step ahead of us. But that's okay. The library wasn't a good place for any kind of confrontation." Declan scanned the Blake's home with a leer of approval. "However, this place is perfect."

"Oh, hello Layla, Declan." Christina sashayed towards them in her southern belle costume. She held a burgundy hand fan and wore a flowing layered white dress with burgundy trim, ruffled collar and a belt. Her hair was in some up hair do Declan was sure girls had a name for. "Isn't the party great?" Christina fanned herself.

"Awesome!" Declan agreed.

"Christina, there you are." Sable came up to her and gently turned Christina to face her. "You weren't at last week's swimming class. Are you okay? You never miss a class." She paused. "Was it because of what happened the week before between you and Zoie?" She seemed worried.

Christina turned to Declan and Layla and saw the curious looks on their faces. She quickly turned back to Sable with an expression more troubled than the one she'd worn a few seconds ago, Declan noticed. "I just wasn't feeling well, that's all. I want some more vegetarian stuffed intestines," she announced. Declan could see she was trying to change the subject. As curious as he was, now was not the time for asking questions.

Before she could leave, they were greeted by another guest. "Well, hello everybody! Don't you all look like you're having so much fun?" Zoie announced. "I think it's great that we can all be here like this among friends celebrating one of the coolest days on the calendar. It's just terrific!" She was dressed as an angel. She was wearing a white gracefully tattered sparkly dress with wings and a halo sitting above her curly chin level blunt-cut golden white-blonde hair. She had golden white sparkles on her face and eyelashes, making her big blue eyes seem even bigger. If Declan were asked to describe what an angel looked like, he would say Zoie. But he knew in reality she was anything but.

"Look what I have here! I made it myself. It's called ghost in the graveyard chocolate pie." She held out the tray to Declan and everyone else to take a slice, passing right by Christina. In fact, she acted as if Christina wasn't even there. Declan could see the fury and humiliation on Christina's face. He felt embarrassed for her. She might not be one of his favourite people, but she didn't deserve that.

"Um, I would like to make just one more announcement," Zoie said in an ever-so-sweet angelic voice. "When I win the seat for chairperson of the Cherryfield Gingerbread Association's Children's Division, which, let's be honest, we know I will," she stated, directing her gaze to Christina, "I'm going to have a party in celebration of my win. And you're all invited! Even you," she said to Christina. "Oh, and you're welcome! Enjoy!" She then slithered off like the snake that she truly was.

"What a witch!" Layla whispered.

"Yeah, that too!" Declan agreed.

✐ Betrayal of a Friend

At the buffet table, Samantha scooped bloody beetle juice into a skull glass while talking with Regan and his older sister Lynette. She was dressed as a princess wearing a long emerald-green satin dress with white inlet, bell sleeves with gold trim at the seams and a matching headpiece resting on top of her fiery red hair that she wore in a similar style to Christina's.

Declan had shared nothing with Samantha about his findings after he questioned her again, in fear she would take it upon herself to rescue the cookie, potentially causing it harm and blowing the case. *She'll know soon enough,* he thought. He only hoped they weren't too late.

"Sam, are you still worried you'll never see the gingerbread penguin again?" Declan heard Regan ask as he approached them.

"Of course I am!" a nervous Samantha answered, clutching her glass fiercely with both hands. "You didn't see that last letter I received or the one Declan got. I just don't know what this person is capable of. I won't relax until the cookie is in my hands."

"You did your part," Regan reminded her as he adjusted his army commando helmet. "You left the recipe in the library just like you were asked. I'm sure you'll be contacted soon about where you can pick it up."

"I don't know if keeping your word matters to this person." Samantha looked down into her glass. "If who ever did this could do this to their best friend, how can I trust anything they say as truthful?"

"Exactly," Declan interrupted. "Two days has gone by since you dropped the recipe off at the library, yet you've had no contact about where to pick up the cookie. For all we know the cookie could be crushed into a million little crumbs."

"Oh, Sam, don't," Lynette begged, as she saw water swell up in Samantha's eyes, followed by a tear drop on her cheek.

"Thanks a lot, Declan! I thought you were supposed to find the cookie, not make Samantha feel worse than she already does."

"I wouldn't be doing my job if I didn't lay out the realities of this case."

"Lynette, he's right," Samantha said. "I was thinking the exact same thing myself. Maybe the plan all along was to destroy the cookie. Why else haven't I heard anything about it? How am I going to tell my nana, my parents, the Inspire Children to Read Association about this?" She started to raise her voice, causing some of the guests to stare at her. "I will never be trusted again by my parents and I will probably be kicked out of the book club. I don't think I can ever face any of them again." She began to sob and then ran off.

The chatter going on around them came to a complete stop. Addison, Javier and Christina dashed off behind Regan and Lynette to find Samantha.

Left standing there alone, Declan felt awkward with many eyes on him. "Uh...she learned today that she got a B+ on her...um... algebra test." Gasps, ooohs and awes were heard throughout the room at this announcement. They all knew Samantha was a straight A student. "Yeah, I know! That's exactly what I thought. Why cry over a B+?" Declan shrugged then walked off.

❧

Declan found a crying Samantha being comforted by Lynette on a brown leather chesterfield in the Blake's entertainment room. Javier, Addison, Regan and Christina stood around them awkwardly.

Declan made himself comfortable on the edge of an oak coffee table across from the chesterfield. "This case really had me going," he admitted, looking at the curious faces. "Up until a few days ago, Layla and I didn't have a single clue. I actually thought this would be the first case we wouldn't solve. This kidnapping was so brilliantly planned and executed that the only two clues of the case almost went unnoticed." He waited a beat to gauge their reactions and then continued.

"So don't you want to know who did it?"

They all nodded, including the two-faced thief Samantha called a friend, Declan thought.

"Okay, but first I'm going to take you back to that afternoon when it all happened. I'm going to tell it as it was told to me by the four of you and two others. Beginning with the game of Zooloretto the four of you played."

Reconstruction of events at the home of Samantha Tate on Saturday, October 10th as told by Declan McLeod:

"Every single time we play this game I always kick all your butts straight to the moon. Why do you even bother playing with me?" Addison crowed smugly as the game just finished. Christina and Javier had too many animals and not enough space, causing them to lose points, while Samantha came in a very close second.

"Don't worry, Addison. This time I was close. Next time I will win the game, I promise." Samantha started to assemble the pieces of the game together to put it back in its box.

"And I'm a better skateboarder than you are, so ha!" Javier put in.

"Sticks and stones may break my bones, but names will never hurt me," Addison taunted.

"That's good, because if you win again and start showing off, I'm going to have some really interesting names to call you." Christina helped Samantha put pieces of the game in the box.

"Well then, I'll be sure to win the next game. I can't wait to hear what names you're going to call me," he smiled then took a sip of the drink in the glass. "Your nana's lemonade juice is the best! Do you think she'd share the ingredients with me?"

"You can always ask," Samantha answered.

"Maybe I will. And while I'm at it, I might also ask her for the ingredients to the ginger-bread penguin. Ah... I've got to go to the wash-room," Addison added when he noticed the look on Samantha's face.

In a daze, he almost knocked the insulin pen cartridge off the sink top while reaching for a hand towel to dry his just washed hands. He couldn't get that cookie off his mind or his tongue for that matter. He struggled for a few seconds with what to do next, then decided one more look wouldn't cause any harm and went into Samantha's bedroom.

The cookie was lying on the bed inside the same bag it had been in downstairs. He sat next to it on the bed and pulled out the ginger-bread penguin. It was so perfect, he thought as he gave it a once over. What would it be like if his mother had the ingredients for this cookie? For sure she would have her own brand of cookies and would never have to participate in any of those stupid cooking competitions again, because they'd be stinking rich. It would be so nice to have her not travel so much.

If Samantha would only give him the recipe, he could have his mother at home with him all the time. It was so unfair she wouldn't give it to him, her best friend. She'd given him a lame excuse that it was a family secret recipe that could not be shared with any outside the family, because it was cursed. Who cared about a cuckoo curse! He wanted the ingredients. At that moment a thought came to him about using the cookie as ransom to get the recipe. It seemed like it was the only option he had left. Yes, that would solve it. But seconds later he was flooded with guilt for thinking such terrible thoughts, and especially about Samantha. She wouldn't lie about something like that to him or to any of them.

He placed the cookie on top of the bag, forgetting to put it exactly as he found it, then left.

That was exactly how Javier found it fifteen minutes later. He'd lied to his friends when he said he was going to the washroom because of his aching tummy. He had to have another look at the cookie. That was the only thing he had on his mind. No wonder he came in dead last playing Zooloretto.

He sat on the bed and placed it on his lap. What having the recipe to this would do for his father's business, he imagined as he lightly brushed the buttons on the cookie. He would be able to pay off the debt he'd overheard his father talking about to his *abuela* on the phone. Debt he'd acquired from taking out a loan to open up his café, Latín Chisporroteo – Good Sweets & Eats Café, to support the three of them. Before the café, he was a race car driver and one of the best. But when his mother left them, his father said it was too risky for a single parent to continue working in such a dangerous profession when he had two young children to care for, and that it was important for him to be close to them at all times.

He knew it was a sacrifice his father had made for him and Galena, because he'd also overheard his father telling his *abuela* how much he missed the sport.

Getting the ingredients to this cookie was the very least he could do for his father. But how would he get it? He sighed. Sam had made it quite clear she had no intentions of giving it to them because of some dumb curse.

Hey, I got it! he thought. Maybe I should speak with Sam's nana about the recipe. She might be interested in exchanging the gingerbread recipe for some Latin ones. Dad said many non-Hispanic people love our food. They think of it as exotic and different and they love to try different meals so that they can learn more about our culture. I could give her so many recipes that she would become as Latin as my father.

Excited about this, Javier bolted out of Samantha's room in search for her nana, leaving the cookie on top of the bag just as Addison had.

Present Day in the Blake's Entertainment Room

All eyes fell on Christina. When she realized why, she shot up off the arm of the chesterfield she was sitting on in a fighting stance. "I did not steal that cookie! I D-I-D N-O-T!

"Christina, I'm not finished. I didn't accuse you or anyone of stealing the cookie, yet!" Declan said. "Let me finish." He held up a hand when she started to protest. "There's more to tell." And he continued relaying the events of October 10th.

"Fifty minutes later, Christina went to the washroom and then went straight back to the patio, making no stops in between, including Samantha's bedroom." Declan paused. "If Christina had decided to go into Sam's bedroom before or after her stop at the washroom, she would have found the cookie gone. Let me break this down further: Addison left Samantha's place thirty-five minutes before Christina went to the washroom, and Javier left ten minutes after Addison left."

"Declan, I'm confused," a sniffling Samantha admitted. "What is it you are trying to say? Who stole the gingerbread penguin from me?"

"I'm getting to that." Declan sighed. "Between the time Javier left Samantha's place and Christina went to the washroom, which was a difference of twenty-five minutes, someone who was there earlier came back to the house and stole the gingerbread penguin."

"Well, Declan, are you going to tell us who did it?" Lynette asked impatiently.

"Your brother."

✌ Connected

Regan laughed at the accusation. Everyone else in the room was in complete shock over it. That was especially true for Samantha and Lynette.

"That can't be true!" Samantha wiped tears from her cheeks. She was in complete denial. "He left with his mother long before the gingerbread cookie disappeared."

"Yes, he did," Declan agreed. He got off the coffee table and walked toward the oak mantel. "But three quarters of the way through the drive to pick up Lynette, Regan complained to his mother that he couldn't find his insulin pen cartridge." Declan paused and then turned his attention to Regan. "You told her that you must have left it at Mrs. Tate's place, possibly in the washroom. Knowing how important it was for you to have at all times, your mother drove back to Samantha's place. And you knew she would.

"Parked at Mrs. Tate's driveway, you told your mother it was okay for her to sit in the car and wait because you thought you knew where it was and you wouldn't be long. You took with you a medium size duffle bag that was stuffed with something big in a black garbage bag.

"Inside Samantha's place, you explained your situation to Mrs. Tate. She then insisted that she, Samantha and Christina would help you look for it. You told her you didn't need their help because you knew where it was, and all you really needed was a cold glass of lemonade. She then questioned why you brought the bag in with you. You answered that you carry it everywhere. She found it a little odd, but then forgot about it." Declan slid his helmet off his head and put in on the floor beside him. His face was beginning to sweat.

"Upstairs, you went into Samantha's bedroom first, took the cookie out of the bag, placed it in the black garbage bag, stuffed it into your duffel bag, and then went to Samantha's desk and wrote the ransom note for the recipe using her sticky sheets. You then put the sticky notes in the bag the cookie was in. After that, you went into the washroom and got your insulin pen cartridge.

"At the bottom of the stairway, Mrs. Tate was waiting for you with a cold glass of lemonade, just like you asked for. You explained to her that you no longer needed it because you found the cartridge and that you took your insulin shot upstairs. You then left. Did I miss anything?" Declan asked sarcastically.

Regan's eyes turned into slits. "That's a lie. You're a liar, Declan! Samantha, don't believe him! I should have never referred you to him."

"Be quiet, Regan, or else I'll go get Mom." Lynette gave him a scathing look. Regan immediately yielded to her demand. Lynette then turned to Declan. "Declan, please, I want to hear everything."

Declan continued. "I can understand why you would feel that way now that I solved the case. I guess you just thought you were smarter than me. And I have to admit you are smart, but you're not perfect.

"Want to know what got me on the path to solving this case?" Declan waited a few seconds for an answer. When he got nothing, he continued. "Your first mistake was leaving the insulin cartridge in the washroom. Addison mentioned it was on the washroom sink the day the cookie went missing. Although, I must admit, I didn't pick up on this important piece of information immediately. But when I did, it was my first real break in solving this case.

"I was curious about which of Samantha's family members or friends has diabetes and if that would possibly link me to the person who stole the cookie. That's how I learned you came back to Samantha's place.

"The house was full of people. How could you not expect that someone would need to use the washroom at some point and spot it?" Declan asked Regan, walking towards him.

"I forgot and left it there, that's all. How does that prove I took the cookie?" Regan smirked and shrugged.

"You're right! That alone doesn't prove you stole it. Point for you." Declan held up a finger. "But what does prove it is your second slip-up. And that rests with the last two letters you sent out." Declan's voice turned harsh, and his eyes on Regan were unwavering. "You know the one you slipped into Samantha's knapsack when she went to your place for lunch last Friday. I believe you said you would crush the cookie into dust and mix it with the sand at Rush Side Beach." He waited a beat for a response. "Oh, and the letter that really got me going was the threat you made towards Layla, the part where you said she would have a very bad accident if I didn't take myself off the case. I'm sure you remember that one. I certainly do. You almost won. I almost quit, almost."

Declan could see the discomfort on Regan's face. "There was something about those letters that just kept bothering me when I looked at them. I couldn't figure it out. But when I learned you were at Samantha's place at the time the cookie went missing, it came to me."

"What came to you?" Regan seemed confused.

"The thank you letter you sent me after finding Moo Moo, duh," Declan responded as if it was a no-brainer.

For a few seconds Regan could just stare at him. He then exploded into manic laughter. "Is this some kind of joke or something, Declan? You're telling me that your only solid proof I stole the gingerbread penguin is because of a thank you letter I sent you a year ago?" He shook his head in disbelief. "You really aren't the good detective you use to be."

"That's exactly what I'm saying!" Declan took off his wide armband just enough to pull out the sheets of paper he had under it. He then opened the three letters and handed them to Regan to read. All the children in the room gathered around him to read them as well.

"Do you see it?"

The other kids looked at each other baffled. Regan rolled his eyes. "If you're talking about the colour of the font, that's not solid proof. Many people use this colour for fonts."

"I find it strange that many people use gingerbread brown as their font colour, but no, that's not what I'm talking about. Read the very bottom of all three letters where it should say signed," Declan pointed out. "You spelled all three of them as singed. I don't know about you, but that's some coincidence that all three letters have the exact same spelling error and are typed in gingerbread brown."

The kids were dumbstruck. Regan was speechless.

Declan continued. "When it hit me that the insulin pen cartridge could be used as solid evidence, I decided to pay Javier, Christina and Addison another visit to find out if there was anything I'd missed or they hadn't told me. After they gave me a more detailed version of their stories, I decided to pay Samantha's mother a visit to question her. No, I didn't say anything about the cookie or that it was missing," he assured Samantha when she gave him an alarmed look.

"And I guess it was my lucky day, because your mother was there as well. So they both gave me the run-down on what happened. It was then that I thought about those letters again. So when I got back to my office, I pulled out your thank-you letter and compared it to the ones you sent Samantha and me. And that's when I noticed the font colour and spelling errors on all three letters."

During Declan's play-by-play of what happened, Regan managed to inch away from the group, standing just a few feet away from the mantel.

"Regan, why did you do this to me?" Samantha seemed as if she was still in shock. "You don't even like gingerbread cookies."

"I don't, but that recipe is as much mine as it is yours," Regan shouted. "And it's not fair that you and your family get the glory of being the founders of the gingerbread cookie when our family also contributed to it."

"What are you talking about?" Javier asked. "Sam's ancestral grandmother was the founder of the cookie."

"And D.C. Austerlitz was the founder of the gingerbread house. If it wasn't for him, there would be gingerbread families without homes." Regan had the look of a demented person. "Is it fair that a man who contributed so much to what we celebrate today at the Annual Gingerbread Parade and Christmas be ignored in history?"

"You're related to him?" Addison asked.

"We are," Lynette said, still in a daze over what she just learned. "We're his paternal ancestral grandchildren."

"How long have you know about this?" Samantha said.

"A couple of years ago our dad thought it would be a good idea if we all worked together on our family tree," Lynette said. "He said it would be an interesting project and that it was important we know our heritage and beginnings. It took us about a year before we learned our family tree traced back to Nuremberg, Germany."

"But he had no wife and children. How are you connected?" Samantha wondered.

"Apparently he was married and had one son and one daughter," Lynette corrected her. "One night, when his daughter was twenty-two months old and his son six months old, D.C. Austerlitz packed his belongings, left a note on the kitchen table and went. In the letter he said he could no longer live in that house with those selfish, thoughtless cry-babies and that he would never return."

"Child hater!" Christina spat out.

"Don't speak about my family that way," Regan warned her.

"Shut up!" Lynette gave Regan a scathing look. "You've caused enough trouble." She paused for a few seconds. "Anyway, as I was saying, Amalda Austerlitz, that was his wife's name, and her two children lived a very poor life. But when her children became adults, they married and became very successful. They then moved to London, England, with their mother. In time, some of their great-grandchildren moved to North America and here we are."

"Why didn't you say anything to me?" Samantha asked.

"I guess because I was ashamed of him," Lynette responded. "He was an evil, cruel man, our great ancestral grandfather."

"Who your family is is not your fault," Declan pointed out, sounding wiser than his years. "You have nothing to be ashamed of." He then turned to Regan. "You, on the other hand, do," then gave him a questioning look. "Why did you recommend me to Samantha?"

Regan was enraged. "So that she wouldn't think it was me who stole the gingerbread penguin and because I never thought you and your bushy-haired friend would solve the case. Plus, I enjoyed how the two of you made fools out of yourselves running all over the neighbourhood asking questions, investigating Samantha's friends. It was so much fun. Besides, I've never liked any of them and was hoping you would accuse one of them by mistake." He smiled.

Samantha headed straight for Regan, but Addison got to her before she could land him flat on his butt, and held her back. "Let me go, Addison! Let me go! You were my best friend," Samantha yelled at Regan with tears streaming down her face. "How could you do this to me? I trusted you. I told you everything."

"You never had time for me," he yelled back. "You only had time for them," he pointed his chin in the direction of Addison, Javier and Christina, "never me!"

"That's not…"

"And you never told me everything! You never told me the secret recipe of the gingerbread cookie. The cookie my ancestral grandfather discovered. I have a right to it too, and you never told me."

"You never asked!"

"Would you have given it to me if I did?" Regan wanted to know.

"Uh, no, but…"

"See! I knew it!"

"Enough, Regan," Lynette shouted.

"No. It will never be enough, because I've changed my mind. I'm going to destroy the gingerbread penguin."

"Regan, no, you can't do that." Samantha pleaded. "You promised if I gave you the recipe…"

"That was then." Regan looked around the room at the stunned faces then back at Samantha's. "And when I destroy it, I'll put the crumbs a in a bag and sit it on your doorstep, and you'll be sorry you hurt my feelings."

Sounds of music and laughter exploded into the room. Layla was standing in the doorway with a huge bag in her hand. She pushed the door behind her to close it and walked a few feet into the room.

Well, thank the living bejebers. I thought she'd never get here, Declan said to himself.

She carefully put the bag down, leaning it against her legs, and pulled out the ginger-bread penguin. "Is this what you're looking for, Samantha?"

Samantha went limp in Addison's arms. It was like seeing a long-lost friend. "My cookie! You found my cookie," she smiled.

"Yes it was in..."

The next couple of seconds were a blur to Declan. Regan ran full speed, grabbed Layla's arm and then snatched the cookie out of her hands. She turned towards him to retaliate, but Regan had his hand wrapped around the cookie's neck. He then gave Layla a look that told her if she made one more move, he'd snap the cookie's head off. She got the picture and backed off.

"The cookie is mine, and thanks to you, so is the recipe." Regan looked at Samantha as he walked backward towards the door. "If you take one more step, I will break him into several pieces," he warned her as she moved towards him.

"Please don't do this to me," Samantha begged with water filled eyes, Declan thought, yet again.

"It's too late now," Regan said, shaking his head. "You should have been a better friend.

You should have made more time for me. And you should have told me all your secrets, because that's what best friends do," he sulked as he continued to walk, now just a few inches away from the door.

"Woof, woof, woof!" Moo Moo came charging in the cracked open door. The force from the door hit Regan square on his butt and jolted the cookie out of his hands, sending it flying into the air. Declan was too far to save it. *It's going to crash into several gigantic pieces!* he thought. He closed his eyes. He couldn't stand to watch it. He heard screams and shouts and then complete silence. A few seconds passed and then Christina spoke.

"That's so awesome! How'd you do that? You saved the cookie!"

Declan opened his eyes and saw Javier, in obvious pain, lying on his back on the ground. The gingerbread penguin was lying flat on his stomach with one of his hands supporting it. "Wow!" Declan walked over to Javier in surprise over the display of athleticism. "Quick thinking. If you landed any other way, the cookie would be crumbs right now. Are you okay?" He kneeled down to check on Javier, along with Moo Moo.

"I think so." Javier rubbed his head. "Just seeing a few stars, that's all." Moo Moo licked his face.

"You see, I told you I could use your help." Declan petted Moo Moo. "Addison, would you get some water for Javier and a cold wet towel?" Addison nodded and left the room. Declan then took the cookie off Javier and studied it. The details were amazing. "This cookie looks way bigger in person and way cooler," he said to Samantha as he handed it to her.

Regan started to walk towards them and was immediately stopped by Layla and Lynette. "I don't think so, Regan." Lynette got in his face. "I'm telling Mom and Dad on you." She hauled him out the room, with Layla following her.

"I'm sorry I lied to you about going to the washroom," Javier confessed as he sat up. "The taste of the cookie was just so different. I thought it would be good for my father's business, but I would never steal it from you." He looked down in his lap.

"I know that, Javier. You have nothing to apologize for. We're best friends." Samantha laid the cookie on the chesterfield, then kneeled down to Javier and touched his shoulder. "Thanks for saving my cookie, I owe you. And you and Layla, too." She looked at Declan.

❧ Epilogue

"Do you know how Regan's doing?" Declan asked Samantha while she looked over her tutoring notes she'd prepared for him.

"Lynette said he's seeing a psychiatrist." Samantha seemed a little saddened at the thought.

"Oh." Declan felt a bit uncomfortable as well. "Do you think they can help him?"

"I don't know." She twiddled the pencil in her hand. "He apologized to me. He said ever since he learned about his connection to D.C. Austerlitz, he wasn't the same anymore.

"I overheard Mrs. Blake telling my mother that his psychiatrist believes he experienced the same attitudes some celebrities experience once they become famous. That their fame means they're above everyone else and they can do whatever they want without any consequences."

"So he thought that because his ancestral grandfather created the gingerbread house, he was famous?" Declan was puzzled.

"I guess so. I mean, I don't know. I don't understand it as well as my mother. I guess I'm too young."

"I guess so." Declan looked down at the notes he had taken during Samantha's lesson. He then placed his pencil on his steno pad. "Well, I guess he'll be famous soon, now that he has the gingerbread recipe."

Samantha gave Declan a devious smile. "Not with my family's secret recipe, he won't."

Declan raised an eyebrow. "But you gave it to him, didn't you? He said you did, I remember."

"I gave him a recipe, not *the* recipe. I couldn't betray my family, not even for the gingerbread penguin."

"But then why didn't Regan say anything about the taste?" Declan was curious.

"He wouldn't be able to tell the difference between any gingerbread cookies, remember, he hates them."

Impressive, Declan thought. Lucky for her Regan was a gingerbread hater, or else she could have been sweeping up the crumbs of the gingerbread penguin. Instead Layla had found it completely whole under Regan's bed when she went off in search for it. She would have had it sooner if it were not for Pradeep cornering her in the hallway to give his opinion on why he disagreed with the report she'd submitted to the Keep Cherryfield Clean Association.

"Declan, how did you get my mother and Mrs. Blake's help without letting them know about the disappearance of the cookie?" Samantha put her notebook and pencil on Declan's desk.

"Oh, that was easy. I just said Christina lost a family heirloom on the day she visited, and I was helping her find it." Declan reached in his drawer for a package, opened it and then poured chocolate-covered jellybeans into a bubble-gum-pink translucent candy bowl. "I asked if they would recount everything that happened on that day and make sure not to leave anything out."

For a few seconds, Samantha could only stare. "Wow, Declan, you really are clever." She scooped some jellybeans out of the bowl. "I'm glad I hired you."

"So am I." He plopped a jellybean into his mouth.

"Have you been at Dolphins and Penguins Books lately?"

"No! Why?" he asked.

"Remember I told you they bought the gingerbread penguin at the gala, and at a very nice price." He nodded. "Well, they loved it so much that they put in a request to the Inspire Children to Read Association to have a giant gingerbread dolphin made with similar decorations on it, and the same eyes. So Starbright Crystals and Diamonds donated the diamonds and crystals, and Nana and I made a giant dolphin. Both the penguin and dolphin are sitting in their window display surrounded by books for children."

"Sounds pretty awesome," Declan said.

"It is." Samantha seemed quite proud of it. "And you want to know something else? They also put in a request for small gingerbread penguins and dolphins cookies so they can give them out to customers who donate money to our association." She scooped up some more jellybeans. "With the donations we received from the gala and the support we're receiving from Dolphins and Penguins Books, we will be able to continue to grow the children's book club throughout Cherryfield for the entire year."

"Samantha…" Declan said coyly. "Would it be possible to get a few of those small cookies, just a few?"

She smiled. "For you, Nana will give you as many as you like."

"Sweet!"

"But right now, we have to get back to your French lesson."

"Yeah, of course." Declan's cheery mood went kaput.

29695054R00079

Made in the USA
Lexington, KY
02 February 2019